FALLEN ANGEL

SAINTED SINNERS - 1

KAYLA GABRIEL

Fallen Angel: Copyright © 2020 by Kayla Gabriel

All Rights Reserved. No part of this book may be reproduced or transmitted in any form or by any means, electrical, digital or mechanical including but not limited to photocopying, recording, scanning or by any type of data storage and retrieval system without express, written permission from the author.

Published by Kayla Gabriel
Gabriel, Kayla
Fallen Angel

Cover design copyright 2020 by Kayla Gabriel, Author

Images/Photo Credit: Deposit photos: bondarchik, Ensuper, SURZet

This book has been previously published.

GET A FREE BOOK!

Join my mailing list to be the first to know of new releases, free books, special prices and other author giveaways.

http://freeshifterromance.com

PRONUNCIATION GUIDE

This is the story of Kirael and Vesper. Just a quick note about the pronunciation of their names, since I *hate* when I can't figure out how a name is supposed to sound!

Vesper — Vess-purr
   Kirael — Kier-ay-el

1

KIRAEL

Kirael stood on the edge of a rocky outcrop, looking out into a seemingly endless abyss. A few inches from the tips of his toes, the damp ebony rock fell away, and beyond that...

Beyond that was *nothing*.

Like many of Hell's more unique landscape features, this one was designed to terrify and torment. Specifically, it was meant to be a slap in the face to souls who, on Earth, were entirely wrapped up in themselves, in their present circumstances: their possessions, their wealth, their beauty.

Some souls, when facing this endlessness, this misty white nothingness, would immediately fall to their knees, realizing the futility of their existence. They would be reduced to nothing but their fear, their loneliness, the emptiness of an eternity in Hell.

It was an effective form of torment, to say the least.

Kirael didn't feel any of those things when he contemplated The Void, as his fellow Fallen called it.

It made him feel... calm.

The Void was the one place in all of Lucifer's domain that was truly empty. No suffering, no screaming, no one begging for mercy. No one sought this place out, not even his fellow Fallen, the former angels who'd defected to join Lucifer.

Here, he could simply stand and contemplate his own existence, the many fatal failings that led him to become a highly-ranked general in the labyrinthine hierarchy of Hell.

He ran his fingers through his dark hair, then tugged at the cuffs of his black button-up. High-end custom suits were the usual wardrobe in Hell, though Kirael tended toward a more casual style.

Today, he'd purposefully worn long sleeves to cover the angular blue-black lines that covered his arms and torso. Though they looked like tattoos, the marks were full of magic. Spells and wards and incantations, set into the flesh of each Fallen angel, marking them for all time.

The meaning of the marks was incomprehensible to outsiders, but to angels the particular lines on Kirael's body screamed one single word: *DEATH*.

He might be leaving Lucifer's side after all this time, but Kirael was no stranger to death. Assassin, war monger, spreader of fear and hatred.

Perhaps he'd only followed orders. Perhaps he didn't agree with most of it. But he'd killed many, their blood marking his hands forever.

He could never hope to be clean again.

Kirael's wings flared to life, spreading wide with a crisp snap. He could vanish them at will, but he needed them out if he was to dissipate, or magically transport himself between planes. It was much more comfortable to have them at the ready, especially given his task tonight.

Fully extended, his wings were each five feet long. Each was covered in thousands of feathers, white as driven snow.

At the moment of the Great Fall, when Lucifer led the charge of rebel angels, every single one of the newly Fallen experienced an inexpressible, awesome kind of pain. They collapsed to their knees, roaring with agony of it. None of them understanding what they'd brought down on themselves, why they felt as though something essential was being ripped from the lining of their very souls.

When most the Fallen looked up, their wings were slowly turning dark as midnight, the taint of evil spreading until their wings and eyes were black with it. They felt a new kind of freedom, freedom from *His* rules, freedom from the need to do Good.

Not Kirael, though. His feathers were still the very same pure white as the great expanse of nothingness stretching beyond him. A handful of Fallen were untouched by the change. Strangely, it turned those few into outcasts, distrusted by the rest of the rebel angels.

Perhaps that was one of the reasons he found The Void so comforting, when it made other Fallen shiver with silent, inarticulate discomfort. The white blankness he found there still represented some part of him, a morality that he couldn't turn away from no matter how hard he tried.

Tonight, staring into all that nothingness, Kirael felt a strange kind of longing. Of missing something, before he'd even lost it. Unless things went terribly wrong, this was the very last time he'd look upon The Void.

Tonight, he was going to defect.

He was going to leave behind the teeming pits of gasping, desperate souls, the craggy pathways that rose mere inches from weltering pits of lava, the vaguely rancid scent of brimstone invading every moment and every breath.

His wings rippled, feathers stirring in the hot, fetid breeze. He reached back and stroked his hand over the arch of his left wing, shivering at the sensation. Wings were sensitive instruments, and right now they were downy-soft and short, to reflect his pensive mood.

His wings seemed to sense Lucifer's presence before Kirael did. His feathers shifted, elongating and hardening into battle-ready slivers of brilliant iron.

"Lucifer," he said, turning to find the Prince of Darkness himself approaching.

Lucifer flashed Kirael a knowing grin as he floated up to the cliff's edge, coming to rest next to Kirael. Tall and handsome, with sandy blond hair and tanned skin, Lucifer eerily resembled a living Ken doll.

The only thing that threw it off was the fact that his wings and eyes were darker than a black hole, even the part of his eyes that should be white was chillingly, endlessly black. His wings were so dark that they seemed to suck at the air around him, to draw in all the light around them.

It fit Lucifer to a T. He was magnetic, with a darkly compelling sort of charm. And when he grinned, as he was grinning now, it was near-impossible not to grin back… even if he was happy because he'd dreamed up a horrifying new form of torment for the many souls under his power.

"Kirael," Lucifer said in his clipped British accent, looking Kirael up and down. "I can't say I am surprised to find you here."

Kirael didn't respond right away. He felt his hands clench into fists, his jaw tighten, but he simply looked away out into The Void.

"You're unhappy," Lucifer said, crossing his arms and folding his wings up tight against his back. "I admit, I'm a little disappointed, Kirael. I felt we addressed this quite thoroughly. What will it take to end this restlessness? An elevated rank, perhaps?"

"A promotion," Kirael mused. "No, I think not."

Lucifer was quiet for several beats. "I'm afraid I don't understand you, Kirael. I've given you everything you could want. You're one of the most feared and respected Fallen. Your power is practically limitless. Yet you long for something, and I know not what."

Kirael pushed back a lock of dark hair that lay on his forehead and brushed an invisible speck of something from his dark robes.

"Kirael." Lucifer's voice was tinged with impatience.

"You say you don't understand me," Kirael said. "Which is amusing, because I think I finally understand you, Lucifer."

Lucifer arched a brow and folded his muscular arms across his chest, his amusement falling away. "Do enlighten me."

"Before the Fall, we spoke at length about the coming days, about what our new world would be like," Kirael said slowly.

"And we forged that world together," Lucifer said without hesitation.

"Yes, I imagine it would have been nearly impossible without the Angels of Death," Kirael sighed.

"You hold me responsible for that," Lucifer said, more a statement than a question.

"No," Kirael said, shaking his head. "Not in the least. I believed in our cause. I believed that we were righteous."

"Believed, past tense."

"Lucifer..." Kirael looked at him, his resolve growing firmer with the momentum of the moment. "You promised justice. You promised that humans would be judged and punished equal to their sins."

"Look around you, Kirael! That is precisely the nature of my kingdom," Lucifer said, his voice dropping dangerously low.

"This place is nothing to do with justice. It's about fear and torment, all to increase the glory and power of... of *you*," Kirael replied, trying to keep the simmering fury from his voice.

A muscle flexed in Lucifer's cheek. "You disagree with it? You, who rained fire and waged war against a great many of the souls here?"

"Before the Fall, I took issue with the way... *He* treated us, the way He favored the humans, gave them forgiveness for any sin if they merely *asked*."

"And now?"

"Now, I realize that you have created a world that is perfectly inverse. Hell is as unjust as Heaven, but without any of the comforts of home," Kirael said, struggling to keep his expression and voice serene.

"You cannot go *home*," Lucifer spat, bright orange flames flickering in the depths of his black eyes. When Kirael did not acknowledge the truth of his words, Lucifer rounded on him. "You really think you will be allowed to return? Kirael, you perfect fool."

"I think I would rather spend a thousand millennia trying to return to His good graces than another day here, seducing souls into sin."

Lucifer's grin returned, and it raised gooseflesh on Kirael's arms.

"The only thing keeping you alive is my protection," Lucifer said. "If you leave, you'll be openly hunted by both sides. You wouldn't make it a week."

"That's my concern, not yours."

"Who's to say I will even allow you to leave?"

Kirael slid his gaze back to Lucifer, then shook his head.

"If you force me to stay, I will rebel against you. As persuasive as you were before the Fall, I will be twice that. It is your nature to lash out at your followers. One by one, I will silently turn them. You'd never be able to trust anyone, ever again."

"So then I should kill you," Lucifer said, looking speculative.

Kirael's lips twitched. "You're welcome to try. If you fail, though... you lose all respect. Your kingdom will unravel. Be very, very certain before you make your attempt."

Lucifer's grin turned to a sneer. "You would never prevail."

"And you would never take the risk. You know well enough the power of each of your deputies. You might not admit it, but I think we're well-matched."

Kirael watched Lucifer's face heat at the challenge, but he

didn't deny Kirael's words. That was Lucifer's greatest secret, what he constantly struggled to hide.

In addition to being an egomaniac and the most brutal sort of dictator, Lucifer was a terrible coward. Not to mention vain.

The shame of losing to Kirael would be the end of Lucifer, no matter how likely or unlikely the outcome might be. Kirael knew this well, and the look on Lucifer's face told Kirael that he'd played his cards perfectly.

Lucifer turned away, fists clenched. "You will regret leaving my side, Kirael."

"Perhaps," Kirael admitted. "I cannot go on like this, in any event. There is no true choice to be made."

"Go, then. If you attempt to return, I will strike you down without thought."

That much was likely true, Kirael thought. He opened his mouth to reply, then realized he had no idea what to say. Though he'd known Lucifer since the dawn of their existence, Kirael was at a loss for a compelling way to part from him.

Lucifer made it easy for him. Kirael turned away from him, lifting his face up in preparation to dissipate himself to the upper realms.

Faster than Kirael could even process, Lucifer drew his flaming great sword and swooped in, attempting to behead Kirael in a single blow.

Kirael ducked in time, but Lucifer's sword slid through the top arches of both of Kirael's wings, severing and searing his flesh. Kirael howled, dropping to his knees.

Out of the corner of his eye, he saw a flash of flame, Lucifer coming back for a second attempt. He was too slow this time, though.

Kirael managed to beam himself to the human realm, losing consciousness the second he felt the fresh, cool air of Earth on his face.

Then he was in freefall, tumbling down and down...

2

KIRAEL

Ten Days Later

"You won't find it here," came a sultry voice.

Kirael opened his eyes, wincing as he turned. He'd knelt on this ice-cold stone altar for hours, genuflecting, and the sudden movement sent a sharp wave of sensation back into his legs.

"Who's there?" he called.

His voice rang through the crumbling stone monastery, empty except for the vines slowly pushing their way in through the cracks splitting the ceiling and the mice scurrying here and there.

He rose to his feet, squinting through the near-darkness. A single shaft of light spilled from a crack at the far end of the room. The monks who'd carved this temple into the mountainside had lived in complete darkness nearly all their lives.

Those monks were long gone though, so when a woman stepped out of the darkness and into the beam of light, Kirael tensed.

"You should not be here," he said.

"Nor you," the woman said, tilting her head to the side. She wore a tall white head scarf, the ivory contrasting with her coffee-colored skin. Her flowing robes rustled as she moved toward Kirael.

She held out a hand, palm up, and conjured a ball of light. The whole room brightened, enough even that Kirael could see the gentle crow's feet and laugh lines on her face.

"Who are you?" he asked.

"Mere Marie. I work for Le Medcin," she said.

Le Medcin was sort of an intermediary between Heaven and Hell. To hear his name brought up in this context was... unexpected, to say the least.

Kirael blinked. "You know who I am, then."

"Of course. It wasn't easy to track you down, but here we are."

"I want you to leave. This is a place of worship," he said.

Mere Marie's lips twitched. "I think, at the moment, it's just a place for you to hide."

Kirael's jaw tensed. "I'm trying to commune with my God."

"And he's not listening," she said. "He's not interested, Kirael."

"And what concern is it of yours?"

"You are not the only Fallen angel to leave Hell."

Kirael froze, her words shocking him to stillness.

"No?" he asked after a moment.

"Ezra, Lucan!" she cried, her voice thunderous in the small chamber.

Kirael's jaw dropped as two familiar faces appeared on either side of Mere Marie. Two Fallen he'd thought never to see again, certainly never under anything less than dire circumstances.

Is this a trick? he had to wonder. *A trap, perhaps?*

"Lucan?" he asked.

The former head of Lucifer's army gave Kirael a stiff nod, his blond hair shorn short, his clothes oddly modern.

"It's no trickery," Ezra said. Kirael glanced over at the dark-haired man, once a close personal friend of Lucifer.

"No?" Kirael asked.

"No. We all Fell as one, with heads full of pretty promises," Lucan said, his expression dark as a thunderclap. "Ezra and I defected together, after many years of dissatisfaction."

"Mere Marie has recruited us," Ezra said.

Kirael was silent for a beat. "For what?"

"To keep the peace," Mere Marie said. "To keep balance in the human world. Enacting Le Medcin's orders, for the most part."

"And in exchange?" Kirael asked.

"We are protected, after a fashion. And offered chances to assist Heaven, at times," Lucan said. "Though it's been less than a year since Ezra and I came to earth, I feel as though we've done a lot of good already."

Kirael wasn't sure what to make of it all.

"And what, you want to recruit me now?" he asked.

"You won't last, out here on your own," Mere Marie said. "If I could find you, Lucifer will find you. And unless there's something I don't know about, he's probably going to be trying to kill you."

Kirael smirked. "We didn't leave things on good terms, no."

"Come with us, at least for now," Ezra said. "There's no special penitence here that couldn't be found in New Orleans."

Kirael's brows knit. "In America?"

"Better than... where are again?" Lucan asked, looking around.

Before Kirael could answer, Mere Marie cut in.

"What have you got to lose, Kirael?"

His stomach lurched as her words sunk in.

"Honestly?" he said. "Nothing. I have nothing left to lose."

"You'll fit in perfectly, then," she said. "Now, then. Someone fly me out of here, I don't like the damp."

In that moment, Kirael's life shifted with the breeze, heading in a new direction...

3

VESPER

*V*esper Emery stalked her prey down a dim alleyway, keeping her footsteps light and silent. Rickety, rusting fire escapes clung to the building beside her, throwing deep shadows against the sickly pale moonlight that trickled down into the alley.

She held her two golden Tanto short swords at ready, advancing down the cramped alley. She knew there would be no escape in sight. Vesper knew every inch of the city by heart, especially the shadowed, seedy parts.

If you wanted to hunt demons and other Kith baddies, well... they usually didn't hang out at the Four Seasons.

When she was only a dozen paces from the end of the alley, a solid wall of gray brick rising into the night sky, her quarry materialized. The dark edges of the Vesnu demon materialized first, then the whole thing grew solid.

All seven feet of it, including the leathery red scales, sharp black fangs, and eight flailing arms covered in razor-sharp ridges.

"Stand down!" Vesper called. "If you don't resist, I won't hurt you..."

The Vesnu hissed at her, black foam dripping from its

fangs. It puffed up its chest, standing bigger than ever, and Vesper rolled her eyes.

"I'll take that as a no," she muttered.

Then the Vesnu launched itself at her with a growl, and Vesper threw herself into the fight with a whirl of blades and curses. In less than a minute, she'd severed three of its arms and had it pinned to the ground, a blade tip pressed to the main artery running through its soft underbelly.

"Quit whining, they'll grow back," she said, rolling her eyes. "If you didn't want to get orbed, maybe you shouldn't have attacked the niece and nephew of one of the wealthiest werewolves in the whole city, hmm?"

The Vesnu grunted, perhaps saying something in its own weird language, but Vesper just shrugged.

"I guess baby werewolf just looks irresistibly tasty to Vesnus, huh?" She moved back a couple inches, then tsked when the Vesnu tried to move. "Dude, I caught you fair and square. Do me a favor, don't struggle. These are brand new leather pants and I'm trying to keep them nice."

The Vesnu hissed again and shook its big head. Vesper had to jump back to avoid the nasty black froth hitting her legs or feet. She had no idea if the creature's spit could eat through her Doc Martens, but then again...

She didn't really want to find out. She dropped the sword in her left hand and reached into a pouch at her waist, pulling out a fragile glass orb filled with swirling orange mist.

The Vesnu made a last-ditch attempt to rise and attack, but Vesper flung the orb to the ground beside it. The glass shattered, the mist began to seep out, and in seconds the mist had begun to wrap itself around the Vesnu's body.

The Vesnu started to wail, knowing what was coming. The mist sucked at the creature and at the cement under its body. The Vesnu began to fade and sink at the same time, screaming all the while.

And then with a distinct slurp, the Vesnu vanished into the

mist. The mist swirled into a ball and the glass orb reformed, sitting innocently on the ground.

Vesper clucked her tongue as she leaned down to pick up the orb, carefully returning it to the pouch at her waist. Though the Vesnu was now back in Hell where it belonged, a little piece of its essence was in the orb... proof positive of Vesper's completed task.

Stooping to pick up the sword she'd dropped, she gasped when a fat glob of Vesnu blood slithered off the blade and onto her pants. The blood immediately began to smoke, and though she flicked the remainder off her knee with the tip of her cleaner blade, she could already see that the leather below would be scarred.

"Perfect," she groaned. "Of course."

She turned and headed down the alley again, spotting a clump of moss where she could wipe her blades. Thrusting them back into the holsters strapped over her red leather jacket, she reached into her jacket pocket and fished out her cell phone.

"Damn," she muttered, seeing that it was already half past ten. She was late.

Nothing new, really. Capturing demons was unpredictable and near-fatal work at the best of times. Being punctual didn't really rank on Vesper's list of priorities, compared with fighting evil and not getting eaten.

Tonight, though, she felt a little bad. It was her weekly standing date with her big sister Mercy. Though the whole experience would be wretched, and Vesper would no doubt leave feeling much worse for it, she tried her best not to let Mercy down.

Heading out to Decatur Street, she pushed into the throng of late-night tourists, strolling and sipping their drinks as they enjoyed the spring weather in New Orleans.

She thumbed through her contacts, ready to call the driver to pick her up, but Murray anticipated her needs. He pulled up before Vesper in his battered red minivan, the same easygoing smile on his face as ever.

Vesper flung the door open and threw herself onto the single dusty leather bench seat, giving Murray the thumbs up to let him know the evening was successful.

Murray just nodded back to her, his giant white afro bobbing as he pulled into traffic.

"Buckle up, now," he chided her gently.

"I'm late," she sighed as she plucked the ratty seatbelt up and fastened it across her waist.

"I know," Murray said, unruffled. "We gon' get you there on time, just you watch."

Vesper slumped back against the seat, drumming her fingertips against the leather as Murray turned off onto a less crowded street, picking up speed.

"I gotta go watch my grandkids after this," Murray said. "My daughter gotta work the night shift up at Sisters of Mercy. You can get yourself home?"

"Mmhm," Vesper said, turning to stare out the window. The French Quarter slipped by, and soon the bright colors of the Marigny neighborhood surrounded them.

"I don't know where the entrance to the Gray Market is tonight, darlin'," Murray said.

"It's at Spain and Dauphine tonight," Vesper said.

The Gray Market was a massive underground labyrinth of connected bolt-holes that meshed to form a sort of neighborhood for the paranormal Kith community. It held an open-air marketplace, the only supernatural hospital in New Orleans, and easily a hundred other Kith businesses.

"All right, all right!" Murray said, coming to a stop at the intersection.

"Thanks, Murray," she said, handing him a twenty. "Have a good time with your grandkids, okay?"

"Will do."

She climbed out of the van and trotted across the street to

the spot where three cocoa-skinned teen witches stood, smacking their gum and trying to look casual.

The Gray Market was strictly eighteen years and up, but sometimes younger Kith could enter with their parents or slip in after someone else.

"Y'all don't want to come in here," Vesper said to them as she stalked up to a gorgeously blooming satsuma tree, its vibrant citrus fruit in full bloom despite the season. The air around it rippled a little, beckoning.

"Man, you don't know us," one of the young witches snapped back, tossing her long braids over her shoulder.

"It's dangerous in the Gray Market," Vesper said, shaking her head.

"It's dangerous in my hood, I live six blocks from here," the girl snapped back.

Vesper sighed. "Sorry, you're not getting in with me."

She stepped straight into the tree, careful to move quick so that the portal snapped shut right after her, leaving the three girls behind. She landed in the marketplace, amidst a hundred other people buying, selling, and passing through the stalls crammed with an endless variety of magical items.

Vesper felt a little twinge. Once upon a time, her sister Mercy had probably been one of those girls, drawn by rumors of all the Gray Market's mysterious tenants and businesses.

Her lips pulled into a deep frown. If only Vesper had known, maybe she could have stopped Mercy's path to ruin...

Giving herself a little shake, she pushed her way out of the marketplace and into a series of tight side streets. She knew the way by heart, and in less than a minute she stood before the dilapidated old house where Mercy turned up every Tuesday.

"You're fucking late," Mercy said, calling down from a second story window.

Well, more hole in the front of the house, less window. The glass and frame were totally gone.

"Hey Mercy," Vesper said, peering up at her sister. "Can you come down? I don't want to bother anyone."

Mercy rolled her eyes and disappeared from the window. A few seconds later, Vesper heard her clattering down the stairs, then the door swung open. Mercy's dark head appeared first, then her short, gaunt little body.

"You cut all your hair off," Vesper said, her hand instinctively going up to her own head.

Mercy only shrugged, fidgeting with the hem of the oversized man's shirt. It was all she wore, her knobby knees poking out, her dirty bare feet showcasing chipped pink polish on her toes.

Vesper and Mercy were nearly identical, only a year apart in age. They shared the same long, chocolate-brown hair and bright green eyes. Only now Mercy's hair was shorn in a choppy line just below her earlobes, her green eyes hazy.

"You're fucking loaded," Vesper said, her mouth setting in a grim line. "What are you on now? Vampire blood? Pixie dust?"

"Pfft, whatever. I'm high. So what? Quit being such a... a..." Mercy mumbled, pulling a single loose cigarette from her pocket and sticking one end in her mouth.

"A productive member of society?" Vesper asked, crossing her arms.

Mercy snorted, glancing over her shoulder and wandering away from the house. At the end of each visit, Vesper always gave Mercy a little food money, unable to cope with the idea of Mercy going hungry.

Clearly Mercy didn't want anyone else to know about it, or maybe she didn't want Vesper overhearing anything else that went on in that junkies' paradise she called a home.

Either way, they usually walked a few blocks and talked, though Mercy never seemed interested in much beyond earning a few bucks.

"I wish you'd come home with me," Vesper told her sister.

Mercy rolled her eyes and took a drag of her cigarette,

scratching at her scalp. Her hair was already a little matted at the nape, god knew how.

"I ain't staying in that fucking apartment of yours. One fucking room of it's yours, the rest is... what's her name..."

"Aurora."

"Yeah, hers. And that bitch is weird."

The last time Mercy surfaced into the human world to visit Vesper, she'd had a little run-in with Vesper's roommate Aurora. The beautiful, secretive blonde witch took one look at too-thin, shifty-eyed Mercy and fled the room.

"She's not a bitch. She's just... private," Vesper said, feeling the need to defend Aurora. That said, they'd lived together two years and Vesper barely knew more than her name.

"Look," Mercy said, raking her untrimmed nails up her arm, scratching viciously at her skin. "I don't really have a lot of time to talk today."

"Mercy..." Vesper sighed. "Why don't you come home with me, just for the night? Take a shower, get a good meal, I can fix you up with some new clothes..."

Mercy's lips thinned. "Naw. You know I can't leave. I owe my Masters more than I could ever pay back."

"Mercy..."

"If you'd ever been bitten by a Vampyre, you'd like it," Mercy said, her mind wandering. "You'd like it, just like I do. It's... like a thousand dreams, wrapped in luxury..."

"Mercy, they got you addicted to drugs so that you'd give them an endless supply of blood. Which isn't endless, by the way, which I'm sure you fucking know. Eventually your body will just give up," Vesper said, temper flaring.

"I'm fine. I like it here, sorta."

"You're not fine," Vesper said, trying to keep her tone neutral. "You're hard up for a fix, and... I don't know. I don't know if I can keep giving you money. It's like my guilt is helping to put you in the grave. What good is any of it doing? Look at you..."

"Don't be like that," Mercy said, her eyes going wide as she turned to pleading. "Next time, I promise. I'll come home with you. For real. And I'll start saving some money, paying back what I owe my Masters..."

Vesper's heart broke into a thousand little pieces, because for a second she could tell that Mercy really meant it. Not that she'd follow through; it was impossible for her to walk away from the next fix.

But Vesper could see the old Mercy for a second, a vibrant and genuine girl who liked makeup and cheerleading and sneaking into the movies. It struck Vesper that Mercy was twenty-eight this year, and if things hadn't gone off track, Mercy would be going to her ten year high school reunion this year.

"Ves, *please*," Mercy said, starting to look panicked.

Vesper was already reaching into her back pocket, pulling out the three twenties she'd tucked away earlier in the day. She handed them over with obvious reluctance.

Mercy beamed at her, throwing her skinny arms around Vesper's neck to hug her. Vesper was on the thin side herself, willowy since childhood, but Mercy was skin and bones by comparison.

"Shit, Mercy," Vesper whispered, feeling tears prickle at the corner of her eyes.

Mercy didn't hear her, though. Her sister was already turning away, secreting the money somewhere under her shirt, heading back to the house.

"Next week, right?" Vesper called.

"Mmhmm," Mercy said, making a beeline for the front door.

She vanished inside without a backward glance.

Vesper lost control suddenly, turning to kick a dingy plastic garbage can that lay in the street. She felt so helpless, knowing that if she didn't give Mercy money, her sister wouldn't eat. Knowing that what little Vesper did give her probably went straight to drugs and Mercy probably hadn't had a decent meal in weeks.

"Fuck!" she said, feeling the weight of it all on her shoulders.

She allowed herself to kick the trash can a couple more times. Then she stopped, shoulders sagging.

"Impressive display."

She turned to find a tall, dark-haired Vampyre standing in the doorway of the house. His skin was dark as fresh loam, which startled her; Vampyres were usually Caucasian and paler than death itself.

Still, the red eyes and perfectly sculpted fangs didn't lie.

"Thanks," she said, taking a couple steps back. She might be hot-tempered at times, but she'd never take on a Vampyre if she could help it.

He slunk forward, keeping pace with her, and she felt her stomach turn over.

"You are sister to our girl Mercy, are you not?" he asked.

She couldn't stop looking at him. His cheekbones were so sharp they could have been creased paper, his lips full and lush around his fangs. He was incredibly beautiful, in a way that made her want to run far, far away.

"Yes," she said, taking another step back.

He stepped forward at the same time, as if he knew her every move before she made it.

"I won't hurt you," he said, canting his head and smiling. "Unless you ask nicely, that is."

"I'm just leaving," she blurted out. She couldn't bring herself to turn her back on the Vampyre, though, so she didn't actually move an inch.

"I see that," he said, his tongue darting out to caress one of his fangs for a moment. "I am Jacinth. Mercy says that you are a bounty hunter. She says you're very good, and that you'll take on nearly any commission."

Vesper stilled for a moment. She'd never imagined Mercy talking about her, but the idea made her feel a little ill.

Jacinth pressed on. "She says you're saving up to buy her freedom."

Vesper looked him square in the eye, trying not to show her growing anger. "I am."

"I have an offer for you."

"I don't want anything from you," Vesper said, dropping her hand to the hilt of one of her short swords.

"Don't be ridiculous," the Vampyre said, his lips twitching with amusement. "I could drain you before you'd even get that thing out of its sheath."

"I'm leaving," she said, backing away from him, scuttling sideways toward the closest alleyway.

"I'm offering you a chance to free your sister."

She froze.

"Free... like completely free?"

"Yes. That's over one hundred thousand dollars, if you think of her trade as a commission."

"She owes you a hundred thousand dollars?" Vesper growled. "*How??*"

"That is simply her worth," Jacinth said. "The rest is... fluid. Now ask me what the assignment would be."

Vesper drew a breath. "What would the assignment be?"

"One hit. A tough one, but a single task."

"A hit? I don't... I don't do that. I just capture and turn them over to the highest bidder."

"You wouldn't be able to keep this one captive. Besides, we want him dead. Shoot on sight, head removed, the whole thing."

"Again, I don't do that. You're talking to the wrong girl."

Jacinth looked her up and down, then heaved a sigh.

"Very well. It's only your sister's freedom, after all. Probably her life... if you could get her clean, she'd probably live into old age..." He waved a hand, as if dismissing the thought.

"Who's the target?"

"You'd find that out last, after our agreement. Assume he's big, powerful, and dangerous."

"What if I could bring him in alive?" she asked.

The Vampyre shook his head, growing impatient. "You won't."

"But what if I did?"

After a moment's thought, Jacinth bobbed his head. "It would be acceptable."

"You'd let Mercy walk away? No, fuck that. For the cost of what you're asking, I would require you to black list her. Every Vampyre brothel and shooting gallery, anywhere she could score. She'd be total *persona non grata*."

A grin split the Vampyre's face once more. "Now you're bargaining. I like your spirit, little human."

Vesper tried not to glare at him, and failed.

"All right. You've got a deal, bounty hunter. Bring Kirael Lesange to me, and you will have your sister. Forever."

"Kirael..." Vesper said, trying to figure out why the name sounded familiar. "Wait. You don't mean..."

"Yes. He's Fallen."

"You're insane," she said, her eyes going wide. "You want to me to capture one of the most powerful Fallen angels? Isn't he, like, third in line to Lucifer's throne?"

"Seventh," Jacinth said tartly.

"You must be joking. I'm human. He's like..." she waved her arms, lacking the basic words to describe how futile it would be.

"He's weakened right now, as it happens. Lucifer has revoked some of his powers. And he should be on Earth for the foreseeable future."

"Why would you even want him? You can't kill Fallen..." she said.

"Not me, no. Don't worry about my reasons. Worry about your sister."

Vesper bit her lip. On one hand, Jacinth's offer was basically a suicide mission. On the other hand...

"I'd have Mercy, free and clear. No tricks. Right?"

"I'd add in a sizable amount of cash, to sweeten the deal." When she hesitated, he lifted a brow. "Take the deal, Vesper. It's the only one you're going to get."

Vesper blinked for a second. Blowing out a breath, she slowly nodded.

"Okay. I'll take the contract. You'll have to forgive me, though, if I refuse to shake on it."

Jacinth flashed his fangs and winked at her, which made her break into an honest sweat.

"Don't flirt with me, Vesper. I'm starting to like it," he said. "I'll have a contract messengered over to you."

Then he turned and swept back into the house, vanishing as quickly as he'd appeared.

Vesper was left rooted to the spot, armed with nothing but her new target's name and a blossoming note of hope for her sister's future.

4

KIRAEL

"Kirael."

He turned to find Mere Marie standing behind him, having appeared out of nowhere. The Voodoo priestess wore pale purple robes, folds and layers of fabric upon fabric. Her hair was wrapped in a towering fabric bundle, her arms covered in shining bangles, her eyes done up in smoky kohl.

Kirael thought she looked like she'd just jumped straight out of the encyclopedia, her photo pinned next to the entry for "palm reader" or maybe "Vodun".

"You should knock," he said. "And stop sneaking up on me."

Letting the curtain drop, he stepped away from the window.

"I like the getup," she said, gesturing to his jeans and t-shirt.

Kirael plucked at the hem of his t-shirt with a frown. After their first few weeks in the human realm, Mere Marie had insisted that Kirael, Lucan, and Ezra all abandon their button-ups and Brioni suits in favor of a more casual dress code.

Since all three Fallen had defected from Lucifer's army at the same time, all three former angels were going through similar growing pains. Though Kirael and the other Fallen spent a great deal of time on Earth, executing various plans to further the agenda of Hell, none of them had ever been required to blend in with humans for longer than a few days at a time.

"I'm becoming accustomed to it," Kirael said with a shrug, turning to the window again. He pulled back the curtain and glanced down into Jackson Square, watching tourists dashing to and fro in the rain.

"I come bearing a message," Mere Marie said.

Kirael rounded on her. "Why didn't you say so?"

"I am, right now," she said, giving him a warning glance. Mere Marie didn't tolerate snappy remarks from anyone, not even powerful Fallen.

"Well?" he asked, impatient. "Who is it from? St. Peter?"

Mere Marie snorted. "Please. You're all but forgotten up there, my friend. Actually, an argument could be made at the moment whether you're less popular in Heaven or in Hell."

Kirael blew out a breath, trying not to get angry. It wasn't as if she was telling him anything he didn't already know.

"So who sent the message, then?" he asked.

"Le Medcin."

Kirael narrowed his gaze.

"And what does he say?"

"Heaven wants something from you. A favor, of sorts," she said, then shrugged. "They can't ask directly, of course. The Rules, and all."

The Rules, meaning the handshake agreement between Heaven and Hell, saying that neither would directly interfere with the free will of humankind. There were a hundred other little amendments to the rules, minor points haggled over the millennia, but that was the gist of it.

"I'm not affiliated with either party anymore," Kirael said. "Shouldn't I be fair game now?"

"It's not really my decision to make," Mere Marie said flatly. "Do you want the message or not?"

She offered him a single piece of cream-colored paper,

folded in half. Kirael gave her a look as he stepped forward and took it from her, then unfolded it.

Bring me the Book of Names, was all it said. Kirael gave a startled laugh; the task was all but impossible.

The Book of Names was as close to a sacred text as the rebels in Hell would allow. It contained a handful of highly secret prophecies, as well as the names of all the Righteous and Fallen. Lucifer stole it during the chaos of the Great Fall, and he'd kept it under lock and key in Hell ever since.

"Have you read this?" he asked, glancing up at Mere Marie.

She shook her head slowly. "I don't interfere in Le Medcin's doings. I only carry out his wishes."

"What he asks for... it is not possible," Kirael said, shaking his head slowly.

"He wanted me to impress upon you the importance of the task," Mere Marie said, cocking her head. "He said to use the word *forgiveness*."

Kirael's heart skipped a beat. "Forgiveness? From... from *Him*?"

Mere Marie's lips twisted. "I am merely the messenger, I can promise nothing."

"Forgiveness," Kirael said again, mostly to himself.

"I don't know what your task is, but... Le Medcin seemed very apprehensive about it. If I were you, I would move on this as soon as possible."

Kirael nodded, barely listening. Already he was making plans in his head, puzzling out how to conquer the task at hand.

He was going to have to do the one thing he genuinely ought to avoid right now. Go to the last place he should be seen, risk being caught by his former comrades, try to steal a book that was kept under the vigilant protection of a dozen or more Fallen at all times...

He was going to have to break into Hell.

5

KIRAEL

There were thousands of entrances to Hell scattered throughout the human realm, but there was only one in New Orleans. The portal had existed since just after the Great Fall, so there was no accounting for the current-day structures built around it.

Still, Kirael found the fact that it was in a hallway in the back of abandoned Arby's restaurant on Canal St. was more than a little funny. One would assume that the straightest route to Hell would be in a secret temple in the Gray Market or something, but no.

Kirael was able to walk right into the place, the back door swinging in the wind. There wasn't a soul to be seen, not even a rat sniffing around for long-lost curly fries. The portal oozed a dark sort of magic, subtle but enough to make you feel the need to clear your throat, and inspire a continuous prickle of fear at the nape of your neck.

It was a bit like walking through endless spiderwebs; you could feel it, but not see it.

For Kirael, the feeling was familiar enough to almost be strangely comforting. After all, Hell had been his home for millennia. A body could grow to like anything, given enough exposure.

The entrance itself was easy enough to find — a five foot by five foot hole of dense, pure blackness. Kirael walked right up to it, then fished a little silk pouch out of his back pocket. It was a gris-gris charm, procured from Mere Marie once he told her that he needed to sneak back into Hell.

"I am assuming you're telling me this because you need my help," was her sour reply. She hesitated a beat, then held up a finger and vanished before his eyes.

She returned with a handful of items: a few herbs, a vial of viscous black liquid, a little leather pouch she called a *gerregery*, and a tarnished bronze cross.

"This will only work once," she told him, explaining how he should mix the ingredients together and then pierce the portal entrance with the cross. "Appreciate this favor, because all of these ingredients are rarer than you can possibly know. If you do it just like I told you, you'll fool the portal into thinking you're someone else. Someone who's still welcome to come and go without raising any eyebrows."

"Dare I ask who?"

Her lips twitched. "Better not."

Kneeling down before the portal, he quickly mixed the ingredients as she'd explained, then used the *gerregery* and the cross to open the portal for his use. The amulet and the cross heated to the touch, then winked out of existence, one and then the other.

Must be working, he thought.

The air began to fill with thick, sooty smoke, but Kirael was able to move into the portal as promised.

Kirael stepped forward and through, feeling the spell spread over his skin as he moved into a dark, rocky tunnel. A few steps in, he saw another bright flash, and glanced back.

Nothing. The space behind him was empty, and he couldn't detect any presence there.

That didn't stop him from feeling eyes on his back as he headed further into the tunnel. Down, down... he walked on and on until he finally saw a faint light at the end and smelled the sulfur.

When he stepped out, he was in an area of Hell called The Dunes — a cold, seemingly endless desert wasteland. This was one of the very first stops for newly arrived souls, a place where their humanity was completely stripped away.

In the distance, he saw the hazy glint that was supposed to indicate an oasis. Many souls would be dumped here together, still inhabiting the projections of their human bodies. Then they would inevitably strike out for the oasis, usually as a group.

Only, there was no oasis, only a distant mirage that moved further and further away. The sinners would quickly turn on each other, each one coming face to face with the very flaws that had landed them in Hell in the first place: greed, pride, envy...

Being in the desert hellscape brought out the crazed animal in every soul, made them do heinous, unspeakable things to themselves and the other souls around them.

In The Dunes, it didn't matter why someone ended up here. By the time they 'died', which really just meant they graduated to a different part of Hell and some fresh new kind of torment, they could no longer see themselves as good or righteous.

Kirael's first instinct was to unfurl his wings and fly up and out; what looked like the night sky here was actually just a small glimpse of the Atrium, the part of Hell where Lucifer and his Fallen spent the bulk of their down time.

With soaring, starry skies and clouds floating overhead, the Atrium was enchanted to resemble Heaven. But of course, only Heaven was actually Heaven, so the Atrium was always disappointingly cold, chillingly damp, and smelling of sulfur — a far cry from Heaven itself.

After a moment's thought, he realized that he couldn't

exactly just fly into the Fallen's outer sanctum. He'd been missing for months now, and even if Lucifer hadn't declared open season on Kirael, his presence would attract attention.

He turned and followed the dark stone walkway that circled the entirety of The Dunes instead, heading right. Hell was made of a thousand different levels and hidey-holes, all connected by a loose network of tunnels.

Fallen generally flew from one to another, but there were a great number of lesser demons that lived in each level, serving Lucifer in various capacities. Some did not fly, so over time they'd dug tunnels, carving their way through Hell's black bedrock to get from one level to another.

Kirael barely knew the passages in and out of The Dunes, but he knew he generally needed to go upward. He passed the first few tunnels, which didn't seem especially promising, before turning into one whose path took an immediate incline. All the tunnels were interconnected, little arteries spreading vast and wide around the beating heart of the Atrium.

Kirael only made it a few hundred yards into the tunnel before he heard voices. He doubled back, ducking into a smaller tunnel, and waited. Powerful as he was, he wasn't particularly adept at hiding his presence. After all, in his high-level post, he'd never really needed to learn.

Then, his very presence commanded attention and fear. Now, he needed the very opposite. He could fight nearly any demon and most of the Fallen one-on-one or in small groups, but if one of them sounded the alarm...

Kirael didn't want to die under a swarm of Hell's most vicious demons and vindictive Fallen angels. Not today, anyway, when the word *forgiveness* was still ringing in his ears.

He threw a low-level shield up, not enough to put off a strong energy signature, and held his breath. Two low-level Karast demons trundled past, arguing in low, creaky voices as they went past. Their lumpy gray bodies didn't slow, didn't notice him at all.

As soon as they were past him, he slipped out and went on his way. A few long strides down the tunnel though, he heard one of the Karast demons give a loud shriek. He whirled, expecting to see one of them coming at him, though he was still throwing a shield.

But no. Down the tunnel, he saw one of the Karast come barreling toward him, making an alarming sound. Kirael spotted a golden blade jutting from the side of its neck, and blue-black blood gushing from the wound.

Muttering a curse, Kirael held out his right hand and summoned his own sword into existence. The cool, heavy steel was a comforting weight in his hand as he raised it and lunged forward, thrusting the blade into the Karast's belly.

The demon crashed to a gurgling halt, then gave a final shriek as it went up in a puff of brimstone and dust. He didn't speak the demon's language, but he was fairly certain that its last words had been a warning. Which meant that he couldn't leave the other one alive, lest it run off and start talking.

Snatching up the blade when it clattered to the floor, he vanished it to his storage bolt-hole as he focused on the second demon. One small part of his brain was still working through the concept of where the golden blade might have come from. Unfortunately, the realization that there was likely a third party came a little late.

He found the other Karast grappling with, of all things, a human woman. Not one from The Dunes, either. Kirael could recognize a hellbound soul from a mile away, they got this look about them when soul was starting to part from body.

This woman... well, her soul was firmly attached to her body. Physically, all Kirael could take in was that she had a long, dark rope braid, pale skin, and leather head to foot. She held a second blade, something between a knife and a short sword. Seconds after he spotted her, she dispatched the second Karast, severing its head.

It the dusty puff of smoke it left behind, Kirael and the woman stared at each other.

Damn, he did not need this right now, whatever *this* was. She started toward him, determination stamped on her face.

"Stop!" he called, lowering his sword.

She didn't.

"You'll raise the alarms," he warned, but she didn't slow. "I don't know who you are, but I'm sure you're not supposed to be here."

Then she raised her hand, holding a glass orb filled with yellow mist.

"Shit," he muttered. She was going to try to orb him, trap him and transport him... well, undoubtedly somewhere he didn't want to go.

Vanishing his sword, he moved his left foot up and leaned slightly forward, ready to take whatever she was going to dish out. As soon as she was close enough, he threw out a warning: "Do *not* throw that orb. You'll die where you stand, and I won't be able to help."

He saw half a moment's hesitation on her face, then she shook her head. She rushed at him, and he realized that she planned to smash the orb into his flesh. She must only have one shot if she was so unwilling to chance missing him with a bad throw.

"Fuck," he whispered, both his hands snapping out to block the downward arcs of the orb and the dagger, respectively.

He caught her wrist, preventing her from crashing the orb into his shoulder, but fumbled the other hand. She plunged her dagger directly into the back of his shoulder. He managed to twist away from her at the last moment, but she still landed it all too close to his heart. It slid straight through him, back to front, an inch from snagging his collarbone.

"Fuck!" he said, releasing her wrist and jerking away from her so that she couldn't yank the blade free. "Are you fucking crazy?"

She snarled, and he sensed her frenzy; she truly wanted or needed to capture him, that much was certain. He heard a distant sound; no doubt someone coming to investigate the noise and the twin surges of power from Kirael and the woman dispatching the Karast demons.

"For fuck's sake," he said. "They're coming now, are you happy?"

She glanced back, then refocused on Kirael, raising her arm to hurl the orb. Kirael waited until it was out of her hand, then threw up a shield at the last second. The orb bounced off and hit the jagged stone wall, shattering and releasing its mist harmlessly.

The woman surprised him by jumping right through his shield the second he dropped it, trying to get her hands around his neck. He was at least six inches and a hundred pounds heavier than her, which meant her move was sheer, desperate insanity. Even with the dagger through his chest, even though he couldn't move his left arm well, there was no way she could take him.

Kirael released a low growl, grabbing her arm and whirling her around. Careful not to cut her with the very blade she'd thrust into his chest. He pulled her close and got the crook of his arm around her neck. She struggled, scratching and sputtering like a cat dipped in water, but ultimately Kirael was too strong.

He pressed and held her carotid, waiting until she sagged against him and then a few seconds more. She slumped forward, and he was forced to let her fall to the floor with a dull thud.

Blowing out a breath, he reached back and pulled the dagger from his shoulder, hissing between clenched teeth.

"You are going to regret that," he said to the unconscious woman. "Don't know why you'd want to do that, but…"

Before he could even finish his thought, he heard the stamp of heavy boots. Meaning that there were probably some big bad demons coming his way, possibly even a few Fallen.

In less than a minute, they were going converge on his location.

Kirael had a split second to decide what to do with the woman. He got the toe of his boot under her body and rolled her over.

He stilled; now that she was motionless, her beauty was a punch straight to the gut. Long dark hair, ivory skin, high cheekbones and pouty pink lips. She was tall and lean, but with curves enough in the right places. A few moments ago, she'd showcased a stunning emerald gaze, too.

Something about her pulled at him, whether it was her physical beauty, the desperation of her actions, or simply the fact that no human deserved to be stranded here in Hell.

He looked down at her, already knowing that he couldn't leave her here. A human sneaking into Hell would meet a truly grisly end, after a great deal of torture.

He wasn't a good man, that was lost long ago. But he would never, ever leave an unconscious woman alone in Hell, no matter her agenda.

He vanished her second knife, then leaned down and scooped her up, throwing her over his shoulder. Closing his eyes for the briefest moment, he re-oriented himself and then headed for the closest side tunnel, taking right turns where he could find them. Slowly but surely, he emerged into The Dunes once more, on the far side of the tunnel that brought him from the New Orleans hellmouth.

The sky far above him began to darken, the stars winking out one after another. The Fallen were descending now, their black wings blocking out the night sky. Kirael gave up all attempts at secrecy, clamping his arm around the woman's waist as he ran flat-out for the correct tunnel.

He made it in just as Fallen were landing behind him, vanishing their wings and calling forth flaming swords as they rushed after him. Kirael raced for the exit, going up and up, growing shaky with the shock from his wound, with the effort of carrying his burden.

"KIRAEL!!" came from behind him. The voice unmistakably belonged to Belial, Kirael's longtime arch-enemy.

If he had to face off against Belial, wounded as he was, Kiral and the woman would both die horribly. The portal was so close, he was only a few strides away, but Belial was far too close...

Kirael dug deep, found a desperate burst of energy, and surged ahead. As he passed the portal, it seemed to cling to him for a moment, as if the membrane itself was trying to keep him in Hell. Kirael burst through with a scream, avoiding by mere inches a flaming sword whose heat he could feel sweeping up his back.

Before him, the air in the room where the portal lay was thick with acrid smoke, leftover from the spell he'd enacted. He coughed, but refused to let it slow him down.

He didn't stop moving, though he knew none would follow; no one entered or left Lucifer's kingdom without his express permission, and Kirael's pursuers couldn't receive it in time.

Still, better safe than sorry... or dead, in this case.

Kirael ran straight out the back door and around the corner. When he finally stopped, he dissipated himself and the woman, managing to get them both safely to his house before he started to feel truly faint. Dumping her on his living room couch, he dropped into an armchair with a groan.

His shoulder itched as it began to knit and heal. In a moment, he'd get up and put some salve on it to move things along.

For the moment, though, he just needed to lean back and rest his eyes...

6

VESPER

When Vesper first opened her eyes, her vision swam for a couple of minutes and her arms felt strangely weak. Slowly she came around, pressing the heel of her hand to her temple with a groan.

She sat up, finding herself in a strange living room. She was on a silver satin couch, clearly a well-preserved antique. In fact, the whole room was full of antique furniture, dramatic plush chairs and end tables done in dark wood and velvet.

She stood and looked around, patting herself down. She was uninjured, but also unarmed.

Walking over to the window, she peeked out and found herself looking straight down into Jackson Square. She calculated that she must be in a condo above one of the art galleries.

Not exactly where she'd expected to wake up. Well, after she attacked Kirael Lesange on his home turf, knowing that Hell's army would descend at any moment... she hadn't really expected to wake up, per se.

Her mind jumped back to the contract she'd signed, agreeing that she would try to trap or eliminate Kirael Lesange. She'd scoffed when Jacinth insisted on putting in a clause that said if she killed or trapped Kirael and died during the act, Mercy would still go free.

I'm not desperate enough to give up my life for this, was her first thought, but... maybe the Vampyre had sensed something in her.

In the heat of the moment, in hand-to-hand combat with the Fallen angel, she'd been willing to lay down her life to complete her mission... to save Mercy.

Turning from the window, she wondered how she'd ended up back in New Orleans instead of enslaved in the deepest bowels of Hell.

More importantly, she wondered where her two golden Tanto swords were. Made by a true master craftsman and imbued with Fae magic, not to mention kissed by dragon's fire... They weren't replaceable.

The swords had crossed the world with her several times over as she'd pursued some wilder, richer bounties on particularly wily demons.

Vesper heard the heavy thump of boots coming down the hall. She tensed, waiting...

And then blinked in surprise when Kirael Lesange himself walked into the room. His muscular torso and chest were bare, his shoulder wrapped in white gauze. Low-riding dark jeans clung to his hips; his dark hair was damp from a recent shower, just long enough to cling to his jaw and the nape of his neck.

Vesper shivered as she looked him up and down. He was... incredible.

With his heavy black motorcycle boots and the shining indigo tattoos covering most of his upper body, he was decidedly sexy as Hell... and undoubtedly dangerous. Just sizing him up made her shiver.

Though Vesper was pretty sure that Fallen could recover from nearly any wound, Lesange seemed to be moving slowly, like he was in pain.

"You're awake," he said, his voice a throaty rumble. His

ocean-blue gaze pinned her, his lips thinning a little as he looked her up and down.

"Where are we?" she asked, crossing her arms. "And where are my swords?"

"Your swords are locked up somewhere safe," he said slowly. His accent was strange, carrying the distant echo of London, perhaps. "And we're standing in my parlor."

"But why?" she asked, her brow furrowing.

"Why?" he asked, a hint of annoyance in his expression. "I don't know, *Vesper*, why did you attack me? Why were you in Hell in the first place?"

Vesper blew out a breath. "You know who I am, then."

"Mercenary bounty hunter, sword collector. Rap sheet as long as your arm, all earned in the last five years, mostly for aggravated assault and property damage done while you ran down a bounty." He looked her up and down once more, then shrugged. "I got the gist of it, I think. What I don't know is why you came after *me*. I got the impression that you pursue demons."

"I accept targets from all walks of life, as long as they deserve it," she said, giving her head a little shake.

"And I deserve it, do I?"

"You're a Fallen, actively helping Lucifer run Hell. What do you think?"

Surprise flared on his face for a moment. "Your information is inaccurate."

"Look, Lesange, I don't really care. I just take the assignments, I don't really worry about the context too much."

"It's Kirael," he corrected her.

She fidgeted and looked away, having no answer for that.

"I don't work for Lucifer anymore," he said.

Vesper looked back at Kirael, startled. "Sorry?"

"I defected from Hell three months ago."

He reached up to brush back a lock of hair that fell into his eyes, his muscles rippling with the movement. For a fleeting second, Vesper lost her train of thought.

Focus! she scolded herself. *What is wrong with you? Since when have you ever looked a guy up and down like that?*

"I don't really know anything about it," she said after a moment. "Like I said, I just take the cases as they come, anyone who seems like they deserve getting orbed."

Kirael's eyes flashed, but he didn't take the bait.

"Who hired you?" he asked.

"What does it matter?"

"I saved your fucking *life*. I could have left you there, let the Fallen swarm on you and torment you in ways you can't even imagine," he said, agitated. "But here you are, safe and sound. I carried you here, all dead weight. And that was after you stabbed me, if you'll remember."

"Jesus," she sighed. "Fine. It was a Vampyre named Jacinth."

Kirael didn't reply directly, looking thoughtful. "Just out of curiosity, how much did he pay you?"

"I don't see what that matters."

It's interesting to hear what one's worth is in cold, hard cash. Plus, it must have been significant. A human bounty hunter taking on a Fallen angel? It's madness."

"He didn't offer me money."

"What, then?"

Vesper shot him a glare. "Can I leave now?"

"I'd like an answer." He leaned in the doorway, not exactly blocking her exit, but making his intimidating size more apparent.

"I'd like a lot of things," Vesper said. When he didn't reply, just stared her down, she rolled her eyes. "It's personal. He was going to help me get my sister out of a bad situation."

"Ah," Kirael said.

Vesper stalked up to him, getting closer than she should. He could have easily reached out and grabbed her, hurt her, but he didn't so much as move a muscle.

"I need my swords," she said.

Kirael cocked his head and stepped forward, closing the gap between them. This close, her chest an inch from his, she could actually feel the heat radiating off his big body. It made her shiver.

"Think I'm going to hold onto them for a bit," he said, one corner of his mouth lifting in an amused smile. "Don't want you killing me in my own house, little bounty hunter."

The growl that came out of Vesper's throat surprised her more than Kirael. She deliberately bumped him with her shoulder as she made for the doorway, then let out a gasp when she felt him reach out to stop her.

Kirael slid an arm around her waist and pulled her back against his bare, muscular chest. She immediately began to writhe, pushing at his arm. She felt his warm breath at her ear as he bent to whisper to her.

"Don't make the same mistake twice," he whispered. "I won't be so nice next time."

With that, he released her. She didn't glance back, just hurtled from the room, half-stumbling down the hallway until she found stairs that led down to a back hallway on the first floor, presumably behind the art gallery.

The second she made it outside, the too-warm New Orleans afternoon already stifling, Vesper had to stop to catch a breath. Leaning against the building's brick exterior for a second, she closed her eyes and slowly counted to ten.

Something about Kirael... maybe the constant, quiet power that rolled off him. Maybe it was his assertion that he wasn't what she thought him to be.

Hell, maybe it was just how damned good looking he was... she'd never encountered another Fallen before, but she'd heard stories of their near-divine beauty.

Whatever it was about Kirael that unnerved her, he'd really managed to throw her off her game. Hard. She should have gone after him again the second she saw him.

He was wounded, barefoot, and unprepared for a serious fight.

And yeah, he probably still would have trounced her, but it would have been her best shot by *far*.

So why hadn't she done it? Why was she standing outside, hands shaking?

Groaning aloud, she pushed off the wall and propelled herself down a few blocks. She wandered aimlessly for a bit before heading to her own apartment, lest Kirael be following her. The whole time, thinking: *too many questions, not enough solutions...*

7

VESPER

*I*n the middle of the night, Vesper's phone started blaring. She sat up, blinking into the TV-lit twilight of her bedroom, then leaned over to grope the night stand for her phone.

She'd fallen asleep watching Buffy the Vampire Slayer, which was her all-time favorite show. She'd seen all the episodes so many times that watching just a few minutes of Sarah Michelle Gellar kicking vampire ass felt like getting a really warm, familiar hug.

She glanced at her phone screen, which was entirely blank. Some paranormal entities seemed to somehow defy the trappings of modern technology, which was beyond annoying.

"Fucking Kith bullshit," she muttered before she answered it. "Hello?"

"Vesper, Vesper…"

She screwed up her face for a moment, trying to identify the voice. "Jacinth?"

"Correct."

She sat up, trying to focus.

"Why are you calling me in the middle of the night?" she growled.

"Because these are my business hours," he snapped. "And a little bird told me that not only did you fumble your attempt on the Lesange's life, you *made nice* with him afterward."

Vesper's breath caught for a second. "Maybe it's part of my technique."

"To make him rescue you from Hell? Are you playing the longest game of assassin *ever*?"

She sighed. "What do you want from me?"

"I want you to do what I asked, Vesper."

She licked her lips, hesitating. "I don't think I can. He's too strong."

"That's too bad," Jacinth said, his tone going flat. "I think you just need some incentive."

"Jacinth, please…"

"Don't bother. I've already sent orders to transfer your sister."

"Transfer? What does that mean?"

"Just that we're calling in our debt now, and she's going to work it off in a manner I see fit."

Vesper's mouth opened and closed a couple of times.

"What are you going to do to her?" she finally managed, her voice breaking at the end.

"We've made a deal with one of Lesange's former comrades. Expanded our business by opening a blood brothel in a new part of town. In Hell, to be specific. I'm pretty sure your sister is on her way there as we speak…"

"You wouldn't," Vesper breathed.

"I did. I think this should really be a lesson to you, Vesper. If you sign a contract with a Vampyre, you'd better hope that all goes as planned. Otherwise, things get unpleasant."

"I can… I can still…" she tried.

Jacinth laughed, a cruel sound. "Don't bother. I'm not even going to pretend to give you another shot. You've angered me."

There was a sudden click.

"Hello? Jacinth?" she asked, but he'd hung up. "Son of a BITCH!"

She dropped the phone onto the bed and lay back. A soft knock at her door, Aurora's soft voice on the other side.

"I'm fine!" Vesper shouted, and then she lay still until she heard her roommate's retreating footsteps.

But she wasn't fine, not in the least. She picked up her phone and tried to call Mercy, wondering if maybe Jacinth was just trying to scare her. She jumped when she heard the three-tone blare come across the line.

"You've reached a number that has been disconnected," a voice told her.

"Shit," she said, staring up into the darkness.

How in the Hell have I managed to actually make Mercy's life worse than it already was?

And then, *Now I either have to kill a fucking Fallen angel, or break into Hell and steal my sister back.*

She reached over and flicked on the lamp sitting on her bedside table, then shoved back the covers and got to her feet. With this much on her mind, sleep would be impossible...

She either needed to know how to kill Kirael, or how to get into Hell without Jacinth's help. The answers weren't going to appear here in her room, but the Twilight Library in the Grey Market would be a good starting point.

Looking at her watch, she groaned and started to dress.

Life was about to get really, really difficult from here on out.

8

VESPER

Slamming yet another book shut and tossing into the haphazard pile collecting on her library desk, Vesper stood up and gave herself a shake. The cavernous, dusty library was practically empty — this was the time of night that Kith were the most active, so it made sense.

Finding the answers she needed was proving impossible. Or rather, she was finding the answers, but they weren't what she needed to know.

Killing Kirael was out of the question. She'd need to have the flaming sword from another Fallen, someone at least as powerful as he was. She'd need to cleave his head from his shoulders and pierce his heart, then do some insane-sounding ritual to send his soul spiraling away.

She'd have to make him cease to exist, basically... plus, it would take her months to gather the needed equipment, at the very least.

And if she were to be completely honest with herself, Vesper didn't have it in her heart to banish someone's *soul*.

Nor could she seriously consider killing Kirael. It would be a damned shame to kill a man that good-looking, in the rare event that he didn't kill her first once she attacked him.

That left breaking into Hell, which was a truly Herculean task. Apparently Hell had quite a sensitive system that detected the entrance and exit of every person, and it was quite difficult to fool.

The methods of trickery to effectively enter Hell broke down into three categories: complex potions with bizarre ingredients, various types of body metamorphosis, and kidnapping or blackmail.

None of those options were particularly accessible to Vesper at the moment.

Ergo, she was in a pretty tight spot. Scooping up the whole armful of books, nearly staggering under their weight, she carried them to the return cart. She stomped out of the library, brushing past the unmanned circulation desk, then pulled out her cell phone.

Thumbing through her contacts list, she realized that she really only had one option at this point: she needed to head to Crane and Co. Being a freelance employee, Vesper hardly ever went into the office, but her employer might at least be able to give her a starting point.

She trudged seven blocks east, passing through the marketplace and into a small side street of service-oriented businesses. Witch doctors, exorcists, and practitioners of Kith law.

Emerson Crane was the latter, a Kith lawyer who took on all sorts of different cases and assignments. If, in the course of those proceedings, someone needed a private eye or needed someone hunted down and orbed... that was where Vesper came in.

A bell tinkled as she pushed open the heavy front door and made her way into the office. The front room was stuffed to the gills with stacks of cluttered, dusty files.

Vargus, her half-feral werewolf of a coworker, was sitting at the sole desk and chair. Well, if you considered feet up on the desk, leaning back and taking a nice long nap *sitting*. Between his enormous seven foot frame and the fact that he was permanently half-shifted between human and wolf, he generally terrified anyone seeing him for the first time.

When Vesper introduced herself at their first meeting and shook his hand, unflinching, she'd somehow managed to make herself a friend for life. A grumpy, mostly insane friend who scared everyone in his path. But still...

"Hey," she said, slapping the bare sole of his foot.

He startled awake, sweeping a stack of files to the floor as he scrabbled to get himself upright. A little cloud of dust rose, making Vesper cough as she waved it out of her face.

"Wha? Urmph," Vargus said, rubbing at his eyes.

"I need to talk to Crane," Vesper said. She didn't bother to ask if he was in; Emerson Crane arrived promptly at five p.m. every day and left at exactly three a.m. He liked rules and order. And above all else, he believed in the power of a good *schedule*.

"Mmmkay," Vargus said. Then he raised his voice and shouted through the door into the back office. "Crane! Vesper's here!"

When no response was particularly forthcoming, Vargus shrugged and waved Vesper on. Vargus was no legal eagle; his job at Crane and Co. was that of bodyguard. For being slow and prone to random naps, Vargus was astonishingly quick and effective when it came to necessary violence.

Vesper swept through into the back office, which was every bit as spotlessly tidy as the front office was chaotic. Crane was sitting at his pristine desk, looking down his nose over his reading glasses at a sheaf of legal documents. His white hair was neatly parted, his tweed suit immaculate.

When Vesper entered, he took off his glasses and stood. Polite nearly to a fault, he gave Vesper a little bow before falling back into his chair with a sigh. He moved as slow as molasses, which drove Vesper crazy, but then again he was the oldest living creature she'd ever met.

"This is an unexpected visit," he said, eyeing her curiously as he checked the time on his pocket watch.

Vesper's lips twitched. "I need a favor. Or perhaps some advice."

"Oh?" he asked, his brows rising with surprise. "I suppose there's a first time for everything."

Vesper had the good grace to flush a little. Sure, she could be a little... opinionated. She generally meant well, even if she could be more than a little gruff about it.

"Do you mind?" she asked.

"Sure, sure," he said, gesturing to the empty chair across from his desk. "Sit, please."

Vesper rested her butt on the arm of the chair, earning a disdainful look from Crane.

"I need to sneak into Hell," she said.

Crane gave her a perfectly blank look, blinking. "Excuse me?"

"You know the situation with my sister," she said.

Crane nodded.

"Well... one of her bosses offered me a trade. My sister, in exchange for running down a particularly tough bounty."

"I'm almost afraid to ask," he sighed.

"Kirael Lesange."

Crane straightened. "Isn't he..."

"Fallen, yeah."

Her boss dropped his head, pinching the bridge of his nose for a few moments before speaking again.

"You didn't take it, I hope," he said, though his tone said he knew just what she'd done.

"I did."

"And, presumably, you neither killed him nor died," Crane surmised. "A draw, in your book."

"But now the Vampyre who contracted me is very, very angry. And he's taking it out on Mercy, moving her to a blood brothel in Hell, someplace I can't even visit her to make sure she's all right."

Crane stood abruptly. He began pacing the room, muttering

to himself. Vesper stayed quiet for a few minutes, letting him think it all through. When he stopped and turned to her, the look on his face wasn't what she'd call hopeful.

"Have you any friends who are advanced practitioners of Voodoo?" he asked.

"No."

"Do you know any dragons?"

"What? No. Do dragons still exist? I thought they were extinct," she said, wrinkling her nose.

Crane waved her question away. "I will assume you've already considered trying to shapeshift."

"I can't acquire that skill in a reasonable amount of time, so... that's out."

"There's really only one quick way in, as far as I can tell."

Vesper stood. "Tell me. That's what I'm here to find out."

"Well... I'm not sure it's viable." He paused. "Exactly how angry did you make the Fallen angel?"

Vesper was rooted to the spot, her brain whirling, trying to piece together a possible avenue for rescuing her sister.

"Umm... not too angry, maybe?" she guessed.

Crane gave her a stern look.

"All right, I stabbed him, but he didn't seem that mad about it," she confessed.

Crane closed his eyes for a moment, exhaling deeply.

"Vesper, I suggest that you go about trying to make amends, and quickly. Even better, if I were you I would be trying to figure out what you can offer him to help you."

"I don't know a thing about him," she said, her lips twisting.

"You're a part-time private eye. I'm sure you can work something out, no?" Crane asked, shuffling over to retake his seat.

"Right," she said, nodding. "Yeah. Okay. Thanks."

"I'm here if you need me," he said. When he glanced down at the papers on his desk once more, she took it as a dismissal and headed back out into the front office.

"How'd it go?" Vargus asked, not looking up from the Times Picayune newspaper he held.

"Good, kind of. How do you feel about doing a little profiling for me?"

He folded down the paper to glance at her, and she tried not to snort aloud when she saw he was reading the comics.

"Anyone interesting?" he asked.

"Oh, you know. Just your usual Fallen…"

"What? Tell me everything!" he said. Gossip was Vargus's very favorite thing. Next to naps, at least.

"Clear off somewhere for me to sit, and we can hatch a plan," Vesper said. "I need your help figuring out his whole story, and any weaknesses I can exploit."

"Vesper, I love it when you talk all aggressive to me," Vargus said with a toothy grin.

As Vargus jumped up and started moving files around, a smile tugged her lips for the first time since Jacinth's phone call.

Maybe, just *maybe* she could fix this…

9
VESPER

Vesper flipped through what felt like the thousandth musty old scroll, squinting to make out the contents.

"Archangels through the ages..." she read aloud to herself. "Ugh, useless."

She shoved the book away and yawned. Looking at her watch, she tried to decide whether she needed more coffee or some water to balance out the zillion cups she'd already guzzled down.

She didn't want to attract any more attention to herself, since she was already accompanied by a seven foot tall hairy man in a suit. Coupled with her resting bitch face, head-to-toe leather outfit, and the katana on her back... they were turning a lot of heads.

"Hey," Vargus said, poking his head into the cramped back room of the library that Vesper had staked out as her territory for the last two days. "I think I might have something."

"Really?" Vesper said, perking up a little.

"Well... you aren't going to love it, probably," he said, fidgeting.

Vesper sat back in her chair, giving him a long look. "Go on..."

"Remember the time that Laagos demon camped out in your apartment and tried to kill you?"

Vesper canted her head. "Yeah."

"And I came over to help you roust it, which was... interesting."

Vesper sighed. "Yeah. I really liked that couch, but it was burned beyond reckoning."

"Right. And then, for the briefest moment, I met your lovely roommate."

"Oh, yeah..." Vesper said with a snort. "You were ridiculously awestruck. I woulda thought you were meeting a celebrity or something."

"As I told you before," Vargus said, looking annoyed. "It was not her beauty."

"Suuuure."

"Vesper... she's a Null."

Vesper stood and stretched. "I don't know what that means, dude."

"Have you ever sussed out what kind of Kith she is?"

Vesper paused. "White witch, I think."

"Nope."

"What's a Null?"

"Someone who's magically... blank. She's the center line between Heaven and Hell, someone born with the specific goal of settling debts between the two kingdoms."

"So?"

"So... have you read a lot of end-of-the-world prophecy?"

"Assume that I have a life and therefore haven't read *any*," Vesper said, beginning to lose patience.

"In many doomsday prophecies, a small collection of Nulls side with either Heaven or Hell. Eventually they decide whether Heaven or Hell wins the eternal war."

Vesper squinted at him, trying to make sense of his words. "What?"

"In this... interpretation, Heaven and Hell are playing against each other. The game is complex, as elaborate as..." he paused. "Well, as the entirety of humanity, I guess."

"And the Nulls... what, choose sides?"

"More like they're... convinced. By the righteousness of Heaven, or the lavish comforts of Hell. Either way, whichever side ends up with the most Nulls will sort of... win."

Vesper took a second. "Okay, one: I don't like the word win used in this scenario. Two, that makes Nulls sound pretty damned important."

"They are. And it just so happens that your roommate is one."

Vesper gave him a long look. "You're crazy."

"I'm not, I swear it."

"How do you know? How long have you known?"

"I met her when I ran into you both at the market, remember?"

"Yeah, I guess."

"Well, the second I looked at her, every hair on my body shot straight out. I knew she was unusual, I just didn't know what kind of unusual. And it took me months to figure it out." He gave her something close to a bashful look. "I researched it in my free time."

"Nerd."

"And yet, you choose to hang out with me," Vargus pointed out.

Vesper blew out a breath.

"Okay... well... If she's such a hot commodity, why would she be hiding out, living in some cramped apartment with me?"

Vargus shrugged. "Beats me. Trying to avoid being tempted by Lucifer, maybe?"

"Well... even if she is what you say—"

"She is," he cut in.

"Even if she is, I don't really see your point."

"Ah! Right," he said, walking over to unfurl a parchment on the table. "Right... here."

She took a few moments to read the parchment, trying to parse the ancient text.

"...shall search for a void, above all else..." she read, then looked up at Vargas.

"Null and void," he said with a shrug. "Same thing."

"So... Heaven and Hell would both be very, very interested in the location of a Null," she summarized.

"Yep," Vargas said. "That's your shot, princess. Whether he works upstairs or downstairs, I think your Fallen will be intrigued."

"Yeah, but... that would mean selling out Aurora," Vesper said with a frown. "If she's hiding out, she's probably got a great reason."

"Would you rather give up your roommate or your sister?"

The second he said it, she knew Vargas was right. She'd tried to kill a Fallen angel to save her sister. Of course she'd sell Aurora down the river if it meant bringing Mercy back to New Orleans safely.

"Damn," she said.

"Yeah," Vargus agrees. "Sucks, but... it's what I'd do in your position."

Vesper took a deep breath and nodded. "Now I just have to get Kirael to agree to my plan."

Vargus patted her on the shoulder, turning to leave her with her thoughts. "You'll sort it out, Vesper."

She hoped like Hell that was true.

10

KIRAEL

"You're a hard man to find."

Kirael glanced left down the dimly-lit length of Vaughn's Bar to find Vesper approaching. Her long dark hair tumbled down her shoulders, her leather-clad hips swayed. She wore a tattered white tank top, tied up to show off a smooth expanse of flat stomach.

Damn. For being remarkably mouthy, Vesper sure was nice to look at.

More than that, actually.

Hot, was the word he'd heard Ezra use the other day. Kirael was finally catching up on all the human jargon, so he could finally pull out the perfectly trashy human word for Vesper's long dark hair, skin tight jeans, and leather jacket.

Hot as Hell itself. If he ignored the challenging smirk on her lips and the fact that she'd tried to kill him, of course.

"Being hard to find is intentional," he replied as she sat down.

He glanced down at his tumbler of Blanton's Single Barrel bourbon and frowned. He'd just been thinking of her, pondering what to do about the bounty on his head. It was as if he'd managed to summon her presence, though saints knew he didn't need Vesper hanging around, giving him grief.

Just one glance at Vesper, and even Kirael knew she was trouble.

"I didn't know that angels drank liquor," Vesper said, raising her hand to call over a bartender. "I'll have what he's having."

"I'm not an angel," Kirael said, sipping his drink. "I'm Fallen. Make that, *former* Fallen."

"I didn't realize there was an option to leave Lucifer's army," she said, thanking the bartender when he set down her drink in front of her.

"There isn't."

"And yet, here you are," she said, glancing at him.

"Despite your best attempts, yes," he said, feeling his lips twitch with the urge to smile. *Odd...*

"Well... I mean, technically, I was going to orb you and turn you over to Jacinth. From there..." she shrugged and raised her hands. "I just catch 'em, I don't kill 'em."

"There is no distinction, if you know that you're handing a creature over to be executed."

Vesper shot him a look. "Well, aren't you high and mighty?"

"It's important to have a strong moral compass. Especially here in the mortal realm, where there are an endless number of choices. And an endless number of second chances," he said, glancing skyward.

Vesper arched a brow. "You don't have to get preachy. I was just making a joke."

Kirael set his glass down and sighed. "Has anyone ever told you that you have an unusual sense of humor?"

Vesper's lips lifted a little at the corners, but she just canted her head and sipped her drink. Kirael had to drag his gaze away from her mouth, to keep his mind from automatically going to somewhere dark and intimate and breathless.

"Why are you here, Vesper?" he asked.

"Ah. Straight to business," she said, flashing him a grin.

"It's my preference, yes."

"I want my swords back."

Kirael pretended to think it over. "No."

"I think you're going to want me to have them."

"I can't think of a single reason why that would be true."

"Because…" she said, turning in her seat and crossing her legs. She leaned forward a little, giving him a glimpse of tempting cleavage. "You wouldn't want me to be weaponless when we're sneaking into Hell together."

Kirael stopped mid-sip, paused. He lifted the glass to shoot the rest of the burning liquor and slammed the glass down. Then he pulled out his wallet and threw some cash on the bar.

"This has been so entertaining," he said. "Let's not do it again, soon."

"I have something you want. Information," she said.

"I don't think so."

"Yeah? I did a little digging around, and I think you'd be very interested in what I know."

"Well, I'm not." He turned to leave, wanting desperately to get away from the pushy human woman who he found just a *little* too interesting.

And interesting was entirely the wrong word for what he found her, but he couldn't even start to define the pull he felt to Vesper.

"What if I said I knew a Null?" she called across the bar as he strode away.

Kirael stopped dead in his tracks, then turned around ever so slowly.

"Say that again?" he asked, sure he hadn't heard her properly.

"I know a Null. Someone that's been in hiding for years, and probably isn't going to be casually discovered by Heaven or Hell anytime soon."

Kirael looked her up and down. She was perfectly calm and still, her face open and honest.

"You're serious," he surmised.

"Serious as a hanging in the town square," she said, picking up her glass, knocking back the whole shot of bourbon.

Kirael considered her words for another moment, then held up a finger. "Stay here. Don't leave."

"Kay," she said with a shrug, turning her back on him to flag down the bartender again.

"Don't get drunk," he ordered.

She shot him an amused look over her shoulders, her full lips curving in a way that made him wonder just how she tasted. Whiskey, with maybe just a trace of sweetness?

What the Hell am I thinking? he suddenly wondered, catching himself.

He whirled and stalked out of the bar, pulling out his cell phone. He crossed the street, thumbing through his contacts until he found Mere Marie. She picked up after three rings.

"What?" she asked.

Nice greeting, he thought.

"I need you to make some inquiries for me," he said, launching right into it.

There was a long pause. "Oh?"

"I need to know where I would stand with Heaven if I brought them a big, big asset."

Another pause, the sound of an exhale, like Mere Marie was smoking. "Kirael..."

"This is serious, Mere Marie. I think I finally have something they'll really want."

"I don't doubt that," she said in her thick New Orleans accent. "It's just... you of all people should know that you can't buy your way into Heaven."

Kirael paused to absorb that. "That's not my intention."

"Since you've come under my supervision, I've never known you to talk of anything but getting back into His good graces. And I understand, Kirael, I really do. But this isn't a tradeoff, and there are no guarantees."

"I know that."

"I honestly don't think you do, honey. You don't get to go to confession and repent and just be forgiven. You're not human, and... well, you've done something very, very bad."

"It's been millennia since The Fall," Kirael growled.

"I know. But... I just don't want you walking around, thinking that you can go back. You can't, Kirael. You can never go back."

"I don't expect... I don't think I will ever be amongst the Heavenly host again," Kirael said slowly, aggrieved. "I just want Him to know... to know that I am sorry. That I am repentant, that I have learned from my mistakes."

Mere Marie was silent for several seconds. "I can convey your message, Kirael. I just don't want you to hold a torch for something that cannot happen."

"I can manage my own expectations, thank you," Kirael said, trying not to lose patience with her.

"All right. What have you got?"

"A Null, I think."

A pause. "Holy Hell."

"I know," Kirael said. "It's unbelievable. The source is... pretty solid, I think."

"This might bring some unwanted attention your way," Mere Marie warned.

"That's why I'm entrusting you to convey the message."

"All right. All right," Mere Marie mumbled, sounding thoughtful. "Let me make some inquiries. I will let you know what I find out."

"Thank you."

"You can thank me by laying low," she said. "All I've heard the last couple of days are whispers about Lucifer wanting you dead, at any cost."

"Yeah... it's a long story."

"So stay out of trouble for a few days, will you?"

"I'll do my best," he said, then ended the call.

Slipping his phone back into his pocket, he headed back into Vaughn's. Vesper was sitting on the bar now, laughing at something the bartender said. As far as Kirael knew, the human bartender was a normally silent and surly kind of man, but just now he was grinning at Vesper.

"Ah!" Vesper said when Kirael returned to his bar stool. "Jim here was just telling me the most interesting things about how Vampyres secretly run the French Quarter. Isn't that funny, him thinking that there are supernatural beings running around, doing crazy things?"

She winked at Jimmy, who went red as a tomato. Apparently Kirael wasn't the only one affected by Vesper's long lashes and sapphire gaze. Or her perfectly shaped breasts, going by where Jimmy's gaze seemed to be glued.

"Well, it's just a rumor," Jimmy muttered. "Can I get y'all anything else?"

"Another round," Kirael said.

"Oh?" Vesper said, arching a brow. "Do we have a deal, then?"

"We have something to discuss," Kirael said, pulling his best poker face.

Poker was a major pastime in Hell, and Kirael was fairly damned good at it. Still, Vesper was clearly aware of her own... attributes... and unafraid to use them to her advantage.

"Well, then..." Vesper said, hopping down from the bar. She intentionally braced her hand on Kirael's shoulder as she moved to her own bar stool, biting her full lower lip as she went. "Let's talk."

Kirael waited until the bartender set down two more glasses before them, then glared at the human until he moved away to the end of the bar.

"Well?" Vesper prompted.

"Why do you want to get into Hell?" Kirael asked.

Vesper pursed her lips. "I need to rescue someone."

Kirael took a sip of his bourbon, thinking. "There's no bringing back souls from Hell."

"She's human, and alive."

He glanced over at Vesper, a little surprised.

"Is that so?"

Vesper nodded, and Kirael sensed that she was struggling to keep her own poker face on.

"Who is it?" he asked.

She hesitated. "My sister. She's... troubled. After I bailed on your bounty, the Vampyres moved her to a blood brothel in Hell. I've been assured that she won't live very long."

Her words chilled Kirael's blood. He'd been in one of those establishments, meeting a high-level Vampyre who was to orchestrate some important events to benefit Lucifer. Since Vampyres traded in addictions — flesh, drugs, whatever — they were frequent collaborators with Lucifer and the Fallen.

A single visit had been more than enough for Kirael. Beautiful, naked men and women splayed out on velvet chaises, Vampyres and demons feeding on their blood, coupling with the humans whether they were awake or not...

Just the memory of it made Kirael want to shudder. Still, he didn't want to alarm Vesper.

He kept it simple. "That is... unfortunate."

Vesper's brow creased. She traced the rim of her glass with a fingertip, her throat working for a moment as she struggled to control herself.

"I'm gonna get her out, one way or another," she said, staring hard at her drink. "I don't especially want to out this person, the Null I mean. But... if it's between her and my sister..."

Vesper lifted a shoulder, trying to seem uncaring, but Kirael could tell that the choice troubled her. If he were a better man, a different man, this would be the moment when he offered to help her without compromising her.

But Kirael was Fallen. He'd sinned so deeply, so irrevocably, that he'd never be that kind of selfless man again. All his efforts were directed toward repenting for his past.

No time for pity. No time for dallying with humans, no matter how lovely they might be...

"When we were in Hell before," he said, thinking everything out. "Before you rushed in and ambushed me, I was there for a reason."

"Okay," Vesper said, giving him a blank look. She was utterly remorseful, which for some reason amused Kirael a little.

"My point is, I still have a task to accomplish there. If, and it's a very distant possibility, but *if* I could get you into Hell, I would need to split off from you once we were there. It'd be my last shot to do what I need to do," he said.

"And what's that, exactly?" she asked, glancing at him.

"I need to retrieve something that Lucifer stole from Heaven."

"So... you wouldn't be able to help me in the brothel," she said, her voice going flat. He could hear the little bit of hope she'd been building up start to fade. "I don't think that's worth what I'm offering you."

He considered that for a moment.

"I'm willing to guarantee entry. I'm willing to help get your sister out. But we don't leave without the object I need, and that part is going to be a lot harder than extracting a blood whore, I assure you."

Vesper went white, making a strangled sound. Kirael's gut twisted a little; perhaps his words were a little harsh.

To his surprise, though, Vesper didn't lose her temper or lash out. Instead, she got very quiet, a look of steely determination settling on her heart-shaped face.

"Fine," she said.

"Fine?" he asked.

"You have a deal. You get me in, you do your best to help me save my sister. After that, I'm on my own."

"And you'll give me the name of the Null. Before we walk into Hell, so that I can make arrangements in case... you know," he said with a shrug.

She stared off into the distance for a long moment, then nodded. "Agreed."

It wasn't a deal Kirael would have accepted, but then again he wasn't in her place. He'd never had any siblings, outside the sense of brotherhood he'd felt as a member of the Heavenly host.

Vesper turned to him, sticking out her hand. After a beat, Kirael shook it, intrigued by the slide of her warm palm against his own.

"It's a deal," he said, waiting just a second too long to release her.

He turned back to his drink, feeling strangely satisfied with the bargain.

If nothing else, Kirael had certainly just made his life more interesting...

11

VESPER

Vesper felt like she was dreaming as she left the bar with Kirael.

Five years ago, before Mercy ever got involved in drugs, Vesper was a newly minted middle school librarian. Straight out of school at University of New Orleans, she never imagined anything like Vampyres or shifters existed.

Certainly, that fresh-faced, pastel-dress-wearing version of herself could never have imagined that she'd be following a Fallen angel out of some scuzzy dive bar. That version of herself couldn't imagine missing a Thursday night Mass…

Much less celebrating the fact that she'd just convinced one of Lucifer's favored disciples to take her straight to Hell.

Or checking out his ass in his tight, dark jeans as he walked ahead of her, his big body moving with a kind of swagger and confidence that only truly powerful men could pull off.

Kirael led her around the corner to a big black-and-chrome motorcycle. When he plucked a helmet off the back and handed it to her, she gave him a look.

"You're kidding," she said. "A motorcycle, really?"

"Yep. And since you're a fragile human, you get the helmet."

"I don't... ride..." she said, trying not to look as uncomfortable as she felt.

"You want to rescue your sister or not?" he asked. "Because we can't just waltz in Hell. We're gonna need help, and that's not gonna happen right in this spot."

Vesper balked for another moment. Kirael rolled his eyes, pulling out his phone and sending a text.

There was something you didn't see every day, former angels *texting*.

Then Kirael climbed onto his bike, swinging his leg over with practiced ease, and gave her a hard look. "Coming?"

Vesper blew out a breath and brought the helmet down onto her head. It smelled distinctly male, but not in a bad way. *Of course, even Kirael's sweat would be kind of attractive.*

Then she clambered on the motorcycle behind him. The seat was sloped up at the back, which meant that Vesper immediately slid down, her whole body pressing flush against Kirael's body.

Damn, every single inch of him is hard as steel, she thought with a sigh. She rested her hands lightly on his shoulders.

He started the engine and gunned it a couple of times. Vesper couldn't lie, the rumble of the engine between her thighs was strangely seductive. Maybe it was old librarian Vesper that didn't like bikes...

Kirael reached up and pulled her hands down to his hips, then around to his stomach. He said something to her, probably some variation of *hold on*, though she couldn't hear much through the helmet.

Then they were off. Vesper's arms tightened around Kirael's waist, her eyes squeezed shut.

Her mind bounced back and forth between fear and excitement. At first, the ride was very stop and go, since they were in French Quarter traffic. Soon, though, Kirael pulled onto Esplanade Avenue, and the ride got smoother.

Torn between being a little scared for her safety and all too curious about Kirael's warm, muscular body, Vesper tried to relax and enjoy the experience. All too soon, Kirael pulled the bike up in front of a particularly grand Victorian mansion, three stories and the precise blue hue of a peacock feather.

Vesper climbed off the bike first, gladly pulling the helmet off her head. When Kirael dismounted, he stowed the helmet back in the pop-up seat of his bike, then strode toward the house.

She started to follow, so close on his heels that she almost stumbled into him when Kirael paused, then turned back to her.

He reached out to steady her, smirking. Just that touch, simple as it was, made her heart beat a little faster.

I seriously need to get out more, she thought.

"There are a few things you should know first," he said.

"Okay," Vesper said, stepping back to shake off his touch.

He arched a brow, but didn't comment. "There are two more Fallen that have defected recently. We work together, sort of... keeping the balance between Heaven and Hell."

Vesper was startled. "Really? I thought it was literally impossible to defect, and that you were just an exception to the rule."

"Only the strongest Fallen can leave," he said with a shrug, as if being equal in power to Lucifer was just... no big deal. "You know who Le Medcin is?"

"Kind of. He's like... the referee between Heaven and Hell, right?"

"He leans toward good rather than evil, but yes. You could say that the three of us work for him."

Vesper couldn't help but laugh, or hold back the words that came out of her mouth next. "Oh man. You guys are like... an angel squad?"

Kirael scowled. "That's certainly not what I would call it."

"Really? What do you call yourselves?"

"Nothing," he said, giving her an odd look.

"That's no fun," she said with an eye roll.

"Moving on," he said, shaking his head. "Each of us has been given a Task, something that Le Medcin wants us to do. More than just peacekeeping."

"Ah," Vesper said, something clicking together in her head. "Is yours related to this object you're retrieving from Hell?"

Surprise flitted across Kirael's face.

"It is," he said. "But the others don't know what my Task is, nor I theirs. It's a very private thing."

"What is the Task going to accomplish?" she asked.

"That's not your concern," he said, crossing his arms. "I just want you to understand, before we walk inside, that you cannot mention my Task to the others. Not to anyone, ever."

"Ooookay...." Vesper said, pulling a face. "Gotcha."

"The less you have to say to any of them, the better," he said, turning toward the house again.

Vesper stuck out her tongue at his back, but he was already halfway to the front door, leaving her to catch up. She hustled to follow him inside as he swung open the ornate stained-glass front door and headed in.

"Whoa..." Vesper said, staring around in wonder. The whole place was done in stunning antiques, contrasting beautifully with a wealth of African tribal art. Whoever'd done the decorating here had distinctive but wonderful taste.

"Take off your shoes," Kirael told her, bending down to unlace and pull off his boots.

Vesper did the same, still gawking. "This is where you live?"

"No. Each of the Fallen maintains his own residence. This is... a gathering place."

He led her down a long hallway and into a formal dining room, where three other people awaited.

"We were starting to wonder where you were," said a beautiful older Creole woman, dressed in white robes and a towering purple head wrap. When the woman's coffee-colored gaze pinned Vesper, there was a distinct spark of interest. "What have we here? Kirael, you've brought us a guest."

"Mere Marie," Kirael said, "this is Vesper. Vesper, meet Mere Marie, Ezra, and Lucan."

Mere Marie offered a handshake, though the touch of her skin sent an uncomfortable little jolt through Vesper's hand. Precisely like touching a doorknob after walking across a carpet, though this was Mere Marie's magic at work, not static.

The other two didn't move from their seats, regarding her silently. Ezra had dark hair, classically handsome Mediterranean sort of good looks. Lucan was had dirty blond hair and piercing green eyes, and he was looking at Vesper as though she were some kind of strange beetle crawling around the room.

"Here," Kirael said, pulling out a chair at the table for Vesper.

Vesper took it, not missing the look that went between Lucan and Ezra. Disdain? Concern?

The two Fallen were hard to read, that was sure enough.

When they were all seated, Mere Marie at the head of the table, Vesper and Kirael across from Ezra and Lucan, there was a long beat of silence.

"You've brought a human here," Lucan said to Kirael, sounding displeased.

"And she can hear you," Vesper said, raising a hand and wiggling her fingers at him. "You can talk to me, too."

"Circumstances are... unusual," Kirael said. "She has information."

Ezra's dismissive snort was hard not to take personally.

"He's right," Mere Marie said, leaning forward with her elbows on the table. "She knows the location of a Null."

The whole room went silent as a tomb. Tension built as the silence played out for almost a minute, everyone looking at everyone else for cues.

"Can't be," Lucan said at last. "They've all died out, or gone so deep into other Kith worlds that they can't be brought up again."

"I know one," Vesper said, shaking her head. "Sort of... hiding in plain sight, if you will."

The feel of Lucan and Ezra's gazes as they stared her down began to feel unnerving. Slowly, everyone shifted their attention to Ezra.

"She's telling the truth," Ezra said. "Or at least she believes she is."

The angels' cold, imperious attitude gave Vesper a little more insight into Kirael's personality. He might be gruff, but at least he wasn't as haughty as these two.

"Again, I'm right here," she said, crossing her arms.

Ezra's smirk was so infuriating, Vesper wanted to slap it right off his damn face.

"So?" Lucan asked, leaning back in his chair. "What's the discussion to be had?"

"I need something in return," Vesper said, though Lucan had addressed Kirael.

"She needs to get into Hell," Kirael said, splaying his hands on the table. "And back out, presumably."

Another long silence, so thick it could've been cut with a knife.

"Usually humans try to avoid going to Hell," Lucan said, though his tone was mild enough.

"Yeah, well. Not this human," Vesper said, narrowing her gaze.

"She's rescuing another human," Kirael said, then hurried to add, "A live one. I already asked."

"A prisoner of the Fallen?" Ezra asked, his brows drawing down into a scowl.

"A... captive," Kirael said, glancing at Vesper. "At a blood brothel."

"Goodness," Mere Marie said, shuddering.

Vesper saw Kirael shoot Mere Marie a glance, and then Mere Marie lifted a shoulder in response.

"It is what it is," Mere Marie said.

"Why would you not simply... purchase this captive? It is a brothel, after all," Lucan demanded to know.

"Because the price is my death," Kirael said, stopping Lucan cold.

"Lucifer has put bounties on us?" Ezra asked, sitting up a little straighter. "What kind of fool would come after a Fallen?"

Kirael cleared his throat, but thankfully didn't point out that Vesper was *exactly* that kind of fool.

"I don't think that's the matter at hand," Mere Marie said, waving a hand. "The question is, *can* we get someone into Hell? The gris-gris I gave Kirael won't fool them twice."

Kirael and Lucan looked to Ezra, who sighed.

"It *is* possible..." he said, but he didn't sound very happy about it.

"Ezra set up most of the entrances and exits in and and out of Hell," Kirael explained for Vesper's benefit. "He knows all the tricks."

"Getting in isn't the issue. It's leaving again that would be difficult. Think of breaking into Hell like robbing a bank. If someone sounds the alarm and activates the security measures, you'd be trapped *inside*," Ezra sighed.

"Where, presumably, Lucifer would then maim and torture you to death... and that's just the beginning. Once he has your soul in his possession, that would be..." Kirael said, then went quiet. Leaving everyone at the table to finish his thought for themselves.

"We'd need to call in a favor to get you out. We'd need an insider's help," Ezra said.

Kirael snorted. "Who'd help us?"

Ezra turned to give Lucan a meaningful look.

"No," Lucan said, seeming to catch Ezra's meaning after a moment. "No! Absolutely not."

"You want to find the Null, or not?" Ezra asked.

"Nothing is worth that," Lucan snapped.

"Lucan..." Kirael said.

Lucan shoved to his feet, clearly agitated. "I'm not contacting Stella. Just... no."

"She'd do it, for you," Kirael challenged.

"She'd do it to piss off Lucifer," Lucan qualified. "And again... *no*. I'm not talking to that she-demon."

"Maybe you two should just fuck and get it over with," Ezra suggested somberly.

In a flash, Lucan's fist was in the air, poised to crash down into Ezra's face.

"*STOP*," Mere Marie shouted, her voice resonating through the room with unnatural force.

Everyone froze. Vesper, halfway out of her seat, dropped back down and swallowed.

Mere Marie was no one to mess with, that was for sure.

"Does anyone know a better way?" Mere Marie asked. "Someone holding onto a secret Fatale?"

"What's a Fatale?" Vesper asked, confused.

"A being, a female, that can take out almost anyone or anything, if given the right... motivation..." Ezra said. "Provoke a Fatale enough, and it's like calling down a nuclear strike. It just levels everyone in the vicinity."

"So... let's find one," Vesper said, looking around.

Kirael shook his head. "She was kidding. There aren't any more Fatales, unless someone somewhere hasn't matured."

"Matured?" Vesper asked. Ezra jumped in to clarify, his face lighting up as he explained.

"Yeah, they're sort of like a dormant volcano. Everything's normal, then one day," he pulled out his hands, making an explosion sound. "They come into their powers, all at once. I knew one, back in Rome. She was just a normal girl, a servant in a royal house I think. One day I turned a corner, and suddenly... there were just bodies everywhere. Some dead, some unconscious. Poor Alexandria, crying and shaking, not knowing what she'd done."

"Holy crap," Vesper said. "Kith stuff gets weirder every time I foolishly decide to ask questions."

"You don't have to tell us, we've basically seen it all," Ezra said, sinking back in his seat. "Anyway, we're not getting bailed out by some mysterious creature."

"Oh. Got it," Vesper said, sitting back in her chair. Disappointment filled her suddenly.

"Since that's not an option... Lucan, make the call," Mere Marie said, her tone sharp. "I don't want to hear another word about it."

Lucan's expression was stormy as ever, but he didn't say a word.

Vesper glanced around the room. Only then did she realize that Kirael was standing, and that he'd thrust a protective arm in front of her. Shielding her from the fallout, should Ezra and Lucan fight.

Interesting...

"I think it might be time for you two to go," Mere Marie said, speaking to Kirael without taking her eyes off the other two men. "I will keep you apprised, Kirael."

"Come on, then," Kirael said.

Vesper stood up and let him usher her out of the room, not missing the fact that he kept himself between her and the other Fallen every step of the way.

"Where are we going?" she asked.

"I'm going to take you home. I have a feeling that a tonight might be our last chance to rest. For the forseeable future, at least. We're going to need to gather some supplies in order to break into Hell... and assuming we get in and out alive, then we'll have to hide for a while."

"I hadn't considered what happens afterward, I guess," she admitted.

"I won't let anything happen to you," Kirael said, then

scowled as if he didn't like his own response. Truly, it was more than he needed to offer, even for the valuable information that Vesper was going to give him.

As he led her out of the house, silent and tense, Vesper began to wonder...

Were Kirael's motives purely selfish, just wanting the information she could offer?

Or could there be something more? Something deeper, more personal?

Sure, she and Kirael had nothing but a little chemistry between them. But it did beg the question.

Do Fallen ever... date?

Vesper felt her cheeks burn, even thinking the question to herself. Sure, Kirael was handsome and all... but there was no way in the world that a Fallen angel and a mouthy human bounty hunter ended up...

Well, as *anything*.

Get your head on straight, she commanded herself. *Save your sister, keep your head down.*

And then, *most of all, don't worry about the love lives of handsome Fallen angels... down that path lies nothing but pain.*

12

VESPER

*V*esper woke the next day to an anonymous text, presumably from Kirael.

Do you have a formal ball gown? was all it said.

She bit her lip, then replied *No...*

Nothing more from Kirael in the next few hours, so Vesper caught up on some laundry and called Vargus to touch base.

"What's it like working with Fallen?" he asked.

"Frustrating, and a little scary," Vesper said honestly, but Vargus just laughed.

"If anyone can hold their own, it's you," he said before they hung up.

There was a knock on her door around five, just when Vesper was getting antsy and thinking about texting Kirael for a status update. When she opened it, there was a delivery man standing on her doorstep with a package. She signed for the box, which was a surprisingly heavy broad rectangle made of sweet-smelling white card stock.

Carrying it into her bedroom, she laid it out on the bed and pulled off the top.

Vesper's breath caught in her throat. Inside, wrapped in

layers of perfumed tissue paper, lay a formal dress quite unlike any she'd ever beheld. She drew it out of the box, careful not to wrinkle the pale peach chiffon.

Walking to the mirror, she held the dress up against herself. The most eye-catching part was the embroidery. Gems sewn into floral patterns dripped from each shoulder to the collarbone, contrasting with the simplicity of the rest of the gown.

No bunched fabric, ruffles, and organza here; instead, the dress was cut to fit sleekly against the body. It was also backless, in a way that made Vesper feel a bit breathless once she actually tried the dress on.

It was... *stunning*.

For a girl who only ever wore jeans, leather jackets, and Doc Martens, her reflection in the mirror was a complete shock. More so, considering that Kirael had sent the dress over.

Damn. I look amazing in this. I can't believe Kirael picked this out for me to wear... she thought.

Was there more to Kirael than met the eye?

"Whoa!" Aurora said, doubling back as she passed by Vesper's open door. "Holy crap, is that an Alexander McQueen gown?"

The pretty blonde sidled into Vesper's room, looking her up and down curiously.

Vesper turned, feeling guilty at the mere sight of her roommate. "I'm not really sure."

"Where you going?" Aurora said, a distinct note of longing in her voice. Aurora rarely went out, except to visit some mysterious relative outside the city.

Probably because she's hiding from people who'd take advantage of her. People like you, Vesper thought, trying not to cringe.

"I don't know that either," Vesper said, then shrugged when Aurora shot her a questioning look. "It's... a surprise date."

"Lucky you," Aurora sighed. "You should wear those sparkly ruby heels that are collecting dust in your closet. And use some peach blush, maybe gold eye shadow. Make your eyes and cheekbones pop."

"I didn't know you were such a fashionista," Vesper said, arching a brow.

Aurora looked like she wanted to say more, but she just gave Vesper a sad smile. "Good luck on your date."

"Thanks," Vesper said lamely, feeling like a total bitch as Aurora retreated to her own room.

Aurora, whose peaceful life Vesper was about to destroy...

To save Mercy, she reminded herself.

Blowing out a breath, Vesper bit her lip. Her phone chimed, another text.

Be on your front steps in an hour, it said.

Biting her lip, she hurried to get ready, trying to put the Aurora issue out of her mind.

An hour later, she was standing on the street in her blood-red heels, brimming with curiosity. After a moment a sleek white town car pulled up, and Kirael emerged.

He was in a neatly-fitted tux, his dark hair slicked back. He looked like the hottest James Bond imaginable, right down to the black silk bowtie and tall, dark silhouette.

"Holy shit," Vesper mumbled, her eyes widening as she stared at him.

Her body responded immediately, warming and tightening in a way that she found acutely embarrassing. Luckily, he seemed too interested in checking *her* out to notice.

"You look..." he said, his eyes traveling up and down her body several times. "Wow. I knew this dress would suit you, but..." he tapered off, biting his lower lip for a second in a way that made Vesper's blood go hot. "You should wear evening gowns more often."

She blushed, more from the heat of his gaze than from his lackluster compliment. Kirael handed her into the car, every inch the gentleman, and she settled in for the ride.

Still, she could feel his gaze on her body throughout the

ride, making her flush all over. To her surprise, she was a little thrilled by Kirael's sudden and apparent interest.

A ridiculously sexy immortal found *her* alluring? She'd take that compliment in a heartbeat.

"Where are we going?" she asked.

"To a wedding reception," he said. "Have you heard of Jack Darren?"

An image instantly came to mind, a handsome dark-skinned man with a shaved head, always wearing a somber dark suit and a gleaming platinum Rolex.

"I—" Vesper started, then stopped. "*The* Jack Darren? The one who represents all the mages and wizards in the Southeastern states, that Jack Darren?"

"The very one."

"Yeah, well... he's only *the* face of the Kith community. He's on the city council, he advises the Mayor, the Governor, AND the President. Of course I've heard of him," Vesper said.

"But no personal encounters, I hope?" Kirael asked, glancing out the window.

"Ummm... no..." Vesper said.

"Good! His daughter Ammerie got married tonight, and we're going to celebrate."

Vesper didn't quite know what to say for a moment. "How did you get an invitation?"

"Mere Marie loaned us hers, on the promise that we wouldn't cause too much trouble tonight."

"I'm afraid to ask what trouble we'd be getting into," Vesper said.

"The last time I broke into Hell, which you'll remember as the time you followed me through, then stalked and stabbed me," Kirael said, giving her a look that made her flush. "Mere Marie got me through with a spell, but it was one-time-use. The ingredients are no longer available to us."

"And what does that have to do with Jack Darren?"

"He's got some vials of the essence of *la fleur de morte*... a flower that only grows in the darkest, coldest parts of Hell. It's nearly impossible to harvest, too."

"And... that's one of the ingredients we need to break into Hell?" Vesper guessed.

"Correct."

"And the wedding..." Vesper said, fidgeting with the skirt of her dress.

"Is at his house," Kirael said. "So it's our best chance. Mere Marie is chasing down some dragon's blood for us, says she 'knows a guy'. Whatever that means. So we need to procure these vials. Then we have to obtain the cross of a true believer, which is easier to come by."

"Yeah, I bet in New Orleans that's not too hard. This is a seriously Catholic city," Vesper said, closing her eyes for a moment. "Is this going to be dangerous?"

"Not if we're good thieves," Kirael said as the car rolled to a stop. "Here we are..."

He got out first, then helped Vesper climb out before a huge, pristine Victorian mansion. They were in the Garden District, one of the wealthiest parts of town, and on a street famous for towering, perfectly-preserved old houses.

Of course, most of the houses belonged to foundations, or had been cut up into dozens of apartments. Single family-mansions were certainly few and far between in the modern era.

Wrought iron wrapped around the whole property, securing the robin's egg-tinged. three story house. The party was already in full swing, light and laughter filtering up from the house's large side yard.

"Wow, Jack Darren lives here? How rich do you have to be to own a home on St. Charles?" she marveled.

"No idea," Kirael said. "I never really thought much about money until I defected from Hell. Now I'm glad to work for Mere Marie, because I wouldn't know how to go about getting a job."

Vesper snorted. "You, in an office? Nah. You'd have to be a hitman or something."

Kirael stiffened, his jaw going tense. He pointed toward the side of the house, indicating that they should walk around the cobblestone path and enter the party through the side gate rather than walk through the house.

"What?" Vesper asked. "What'd I say?"

"Nothing," Kirael said, then cleared his throat. "Well, I should say, that was one of my jobs for the Fallen. Wet work, they called it."

Assassin, more like, she thought. *Killer.*

"It was wrong," he said, his expression hardening. "I thought I was righteous, but... now I know otherwise. I can't undo all that I did, though."

Vesper glanced away from him, shocked by his admission. It took her a full minute to recover herself, and by then they were walking up to a clipboard-holding bouncer.

Vesper was perfectly happy to stay behind Kirael, though she kept catching herself staring at his ass, wondering if he wore boxers or briefs.

Or maybe nothing? she thought, then immediately wished she could wash her brain out with soap. *Why can't I get my mind out of the gutter tonight?*

"Invitation?" the suited bouncer asked, glancing at them.

Vesper ignored the bouncer, sticking with her own thoughts. Maybe it was the fact that Kirael had shaved his five o'clock shadow, and the result was... jaw-dropping.

She wanted to lick the sharp lines of his jaw, and then...

Stop! she screamed at herself. *Get your head in the game, Vesper!*

Kirael produced the cream-colored invite and handed it over. After double checking the invite to the list, then giving Kirael and Vesper another once over, the bouncer pulled open the wrought iron gate and ushered them into the backyard.

The whole affair was stunningly lavish. Elegantly-dressed

guests standing under a tall white tent, sipping champagne and smiling as a live band played Zydeco music. Couples were already dancing on the floor that'd been laid at one end. Tuxedoed waiters circled with silver trays of drinks and food.

Most of all, strings of lights were absolutely everywhere, twinkling softly and making it seem as if the whole party was illuminated by enchanted fairy lights.

Vesper whistled, her awkward moment with Kirael forgotten. Kirael caught her hand, bringing it up to rest in the crook of his elbow, and led her forward.

They entered the party, apparently having missed the toasts and the first dance, at least.

"Now what?" Vesper asked, snagging some champagne from a passing waiter.

"Mmmm..." Kirael said, accepting a glass from her and taking a sip. "Let's make a couple circuits, see if we can figure out how we're going to get inside."

Vesper followed him, downing a couple more glasses of champagne. All around them were the city's most powerful people, both human and Kith. To her relief, there were few Vampyres. Lots of witches and mages, though.

Thankfully at the moment, the event was less about magic and more about wedding bells; the attention was all focused on the dozen or so bridesmaids in frothy pink dresses, their matching groomsmen, and of course the bride in her enormous white ball gown and radiant smile.

Vesper watched Kirael, trying to figure out what he was thinking without being too obvious about it. She saw him take notice of a table of powerful-looking shifters, each with a beautiful woman at his side.

They were familiar-looking, though it took Vesper a minute to put the pieces together.

"You know them?" Kirael asked.

"Not personally, but I think those are the Alpha Guardians," Vesper said. "The twin Faerie princes give it away."

"Interesting," Kirael said.

"Yeah?"

"I think Mere Marie deals with them in somewhat the same manner she deals with me. They might be helpful, if things go south here."

Vesper glanced at the table again, and noticed that several of the Guardians seemed to be watching Kirael very closely.

"Y'all need a cool nickname like Alpha Guardians," she said.

"I don't think so," Kirael said, rolling his eyes.

"Yeah. Oh, I got a good one. How about the Sainted Sinners," she said, giving him a wink.

"That's terrible."

"Pfft. You have no taste."

"I want to get closer to the house," was Kirael's only response.

"The dance floor kind of borders the side entrance to the house, over there," Vesper said, inclining her head. A steady stream of waiters and guests were filtering up and down a set of stately slate steps that led up to the wraparound porch.

"Mmm," Kirael said. Before Vesper realized his intent, he'd slid his arm around her waist and was leading her to the dance floor.

"I meant we could go observe," she said, her brows knitting.

"I think, if we want to go inside, we're going to need a plausible reason," he said, turning her in his arms and pulling her close as the music slowed, turning from a fast two-step to a slower, more sultry rhythm.

"Uh huh," Vesper said, feeling her face begin to heat.

"I mean to say, we ought to pretend to be a couple. That way if we get caught inside, we just pretend to be in a lovers' embrace," he said.

She couldn't be sure, but Vesper thought she saw an amused sparkle in his eye. Like he knew she was feeling awkward, and he was enjoying every second of it.

Kirael took her hand, his steps sure and easy as he guided her across the floor. The sheer closeness of him was a little too much to take in all at once. She caught a whiff of his aftershave, spicy yet clean.

When she glanced up at him, she realized that he was still a good four inches taller than she was, even in her heels. Something about that fact made her stomach flip-flop and made her melt just a little inside.

Just admit it, you're hot for him, she thought, blushing even harder.

Kirael's gaze was intent on her face, a flicker of something like curiosity evident in his expression.

"You're doing a fine job," he said.

"Hmm?" she asked, feeling a little ditzy.

"Just... I think an outsider might think that you're quite taken with me," he said, his voice a low rumble in his chest.

"Oh. Well... acting, you know. I took a drama class in high school," Vesper said, her lips tipping up into a smile.

"Is that right?"

"Yep. I was in a production of My Fair Lady. I played Ms. Higgins," she said, suppressing a laugh.

"I don't know what that means, but I will assume that you were spectacular in it," Kirael said. "Being such a talented actress, and all."

Subtly, he guided her toward the house, little by little.

They swayed to the music, and after a moment, Kirael spoke again.

"Can I ask a very personal question?"

Vesper blinked. "Um... sure. Shoot."

"You're doing all of this because of your sister, right?"

Vesper stiffened a little, already knowing where this was going.

"Yeah. Mercy, her name's Mercy."

"What's the story there? Why is she... where she is, and

you're... very much not?" he asked. "Sorry, I don't know a better way to phrase that."

Vesper's heart twisted a little, but she shook her head. "It's fine."

"You don't have to tell me, of course. I'm just curious how you came to be a murderous bounty hunter, and she... didn't."

"Well... Mercy and I didn't have it great, growing up. Our dad died when we were young, our mom was heartbroken. She drank, had men around..." Vesper stopped herself, censoring. "Mercy took a lot of the bad shit on herself, to protect me. Drew attention to herself, sort of, so that no one looked my way."

"Sounds like she was a good older sister," Kirael said, watching her intently.

"She was, she really was. But... well, no need to go into details. Suffice to say that all that bad shit, it eventually started to weigh on her. Later, after we were already out of the house. She just never really recovered from it. So she started to drink. And we would fight about that, me and her. So she'd go off on her own, leave for days. And I was this dopey librarian, wearing pastels and thinking the world was fine, that she'd be fine."

Vesper had to stop and clear her throat. To her relief, Kirael turned the subject away from Mercy.

"So how did you get from pastel skirts to black leather?" he asked. "That's quite a career change, you know."

"Yeah. When I first discovered the Kith world, all I knew about were the Vampyres, the ones Mercy hung around. I hated them, from the first. When Mercy dropped off the grid, I got mad. And then I got even... after a good bit of training, of course."

"I've seen you with swords, you're no joke," Kirael said, his eyes twinkling.

"Yeah, well. It took a year of really hard work. Being a puny little human, I have to move faster, hit harder, or some demon will *smoosh* me."

Kirael laughed, and Vesper smiled too.

"Thanks for telling me," he said after a minute.

"No problem," she said, making face.

"Well, I can see that you're not much for chit chat," he said.

"What? I'm... fine... at it," she said, rolling her eyes.

Kirael snorted, then did a fancy move, stepping back to spin her in a circle. When she came back into his arms, he had a mischievous look in his eyes.

"Don't panic," he said.

"What? Why would I—" she said, her words cut off when Kirael leaned down and pressed his lips to hers.

Her hands clenched the lapels of his tux, her eyes going wide at the warm, firm touch of Kirael's lips. He broke the kiss, pulling back.

"A little more convincing than that, Vesper," he said, giving her a look.

"Right," she said, licking her lower lip, trying not to sound too breathless. "Of course."

This time, Kirael slid his hand up to cup the back of her head, his fingers sliding through the dark, silky mass of her hair. He even leaned her back a little, leaning in to brush a soft kiss against her lips.

She let her eyes drift shut, slipping her arms around his neck. Pushing up onto her tiptoes, she met his next kiss more eagerly, shivering when the tip of his tongue brushed her lips.

One of his big hands slid up her hip, his fingers stopping just under her breast, stirring a lazy kind of heat low in her body. Vesper tipped her head back, feeling her long hair shift against her bare skin.

This is dangerous, she thought. Breaking the kiss, she opened her eyes to gaze up at Kirael. His expression was something like curiosity or surprise, his eyes gone a little dark at the undeniable moment.

Heat, tension. A spark.

Vesper couldn't help the image that popped into her head: Kirael, naked in her bed, beckoning for her to join him. Those ocean-blue eyes telling her all she needed to know, telling her that he would fulfill her every desire.

Vesper had a flash of intuition... going down this path would bring her a world of trouble.

The question was... would flirting with Kirael be worth it?

More importantly, did she have the guts to find out?

13

VESPER

She stared up at Kirael, her thoughts beginning to overwhelm her desire.

Kirael couldn't even let her have that, though... the bastard was just too perfect for that.

"You're blushing," Kirael said, one corner of his mouth tipping upward. "Why's that?"

"Um..." Vesper started, unsure if she could formulate a good lie. Kirael was so close to her, and she was half-drunk on champagne and the sweetness of his kiss.

Tell him you want him, a little voice in her head urged. *What's the worst that could happen?*

She opened her mouth, wondering if it would be too bold to invite him to her bed for a single night. The music quieted, as if the universe was preparing for Vesper to say—

"Hello everyone," a woman said into a microphone, which resonated across the whole party. Everyone stopped and turned, Vesper and Kirael included.

The moment between them, whatever it was, vanished like so much ash in the wind. The woman with the microphone, perhaps a family member or the wedding planner, continued on.

"Just wanted you all to know that we're going to do the cake now. Bride and groom, y'all wanna come up here and get started?"

Light applause from the wedding guests. Four waiters wheeled out a silver tray bearing an elaborately-iced white cake with no less than twelve tiers, plus a miniature bride and groom standing on top.

"I think this might be a good moment," Vesper whispered.

Kirael nodded, watching the bride and groom approach, beaming with joy. Kirael surprised Vesper by taking her hand, then he turned and led her toward the house.

Vesper opened her mouth to ask him if he knew where Jack Darren was at the moment, but Kirael stopped her with a meaningful look, giving her hand a squeeze.

Right. You're undercover, she reminded herself. *You're not here to drink champagne and make eyes at Kirael. You're here on a mission.*

Straightening her spine a little, she followed Kirael up the steps into the house, which was every bit as beautiful within as without. All done in a surprisingly simplistic, modern style, the open-concept ground floor was mainly taken up by kitchen and entertainment areas.

"There," Kirael said, nodding toward the stairs.

"Got it."

They headed over to the stairs, pausing when a small army of waiters passed through the room, bringing a dozen or more cases of champagne to the kitchen.

"Now," Vesper said, after making sure the coast was clear. She took off her heels and went up the stairs, listening carefully for activity on the next floor.

She stopped cold on the landing, coming face to face with a long corridor of closed doors and an unamused blonde bridesmaid.

"You're not supposed to be up here," the woman said,

putting a hand on her hip. "All the guest rooms are reserved for the bridal party."

Kirael shifted forward ever so slightly, but Vesper stopped him with a hand on his forearm.

"Oh my god," she said, taking the lead. "I'm like... soooo glad you're here."

"You are?" the blonde asked, looking confused.

"Yeah. Ammerie said her heels were soooo uncomfortable, and asked if I would come up and see if anyone knew where her backup flats were," Vesper said, pulling out the lie with a flourish.

Now Kirael and the bridesmaid were looking at her skeptically.

"You know Ammerie?" the bridesmaid asked, crossing her arms.

"Childhood friends. Our dads used to work together, back before..." Vesper let her sentence drop off and waved a hand, hoping the other woman would fill in the blanks.

"Oh. Well... I can grab her shoes and take them downstairs," the blonde said, tossing her hair. "I'm sure Ammerie doesn't want just anyone touching her bridal trousseau."

"Right. So... awesome. Um... I hate to ask, but is there a restroom I can use up here? All the ones downstairs are full," Vesper bluffed.

The blonde arched a brow, then pointed. "End of the hall on the left."

"Thanks!" Vesper said, grabbing Kirael's wrist and towing him away from the blonde.

The bridesmaid disappeared into a room, closing the door behind her. Kirael gave a low whistle, then backtracked down the hall and motioned for Vesper to follow him up the stairs.

"Nice subterfuge back there," Kirael said quietly as they went up.

"Thanks. If you'd believe it, lying is a regular part of my daily work."

Kirael made an amused sound, but didn't respond.

The third floor landing was entirely different than the second. It presented a single closed door, made of heavy dark wood, every inch of it inscribed with runic symbols. Vesper reached out, nearly touching the door, but Kirael yanked her back just in time.

The runes responded to her presence, giving off a faint blue light.

"You don't want to touch that," Kirael said, looking amused.

"I was kind of hoping it wouldn't be locked," Vesper said with a shrug.

"Well... you handled things downstairs. Fair's fair..." he said, bringing his hand out so that his palm nearly brushed the door frame.

"I thought you said it was dangerous!" Vesper said, worrying her bottom lip with her teeth.

"Dangerous for you," he said, focusing on the door. "I think you'll find that there's not much that can keep a Fallen angel out, if he wants in..."

Vesper was quiet, mulling his words over as she watched him work.

"Ah, there we go," he said. He muttered a word in a foreign-sounding tongue, and all the runes flared blindingly bright at once.

Vesper blinked, and the runes dimmed to a subtle shimmer. Kirael reached out, and the door swung open before him.

"Quickly," he said, rushing inside.

Vesper felt a wash of energy as she stepped into the room. The room was heavily warded with protection spells, probably ingrained in the very walls.

"Whoa..." she said, looking around. The room was large, perhaps thirty feet by thirty, with huge windows that looked down into the back yard, showcasing a moonlit magnolia in full bloom.

The serenity of the scene outside made the whole room all the more startling in its claustrophobic clutter.

Inside, each wall was lined with bookshelves, every inch crammed with a variety of texts so vast it could make some of those kids back in librarian school drool. Tables filled most of the rest of the room, barely room enough to move between them, each table covered with all manner of things. Books, dog-eared scrolls set beside quills and ink pots, a model of the solar system, a basket of withered fruit, more books.

There were little glass jars everywhere, filled with all sorts of things: pencils sharpened almost down to nubs, bits of ribbon, loose buttons, marbles, tubes of paint.

Vesper felt for all the world as though she'd just stepped into DaVinci's workshop.

"Right. We've probably only got a few minutes before the spell wears off and Darren knows we're in here," Kirael said, looking around.

"Do you need my help looking?" Vesper asked.

Kirael was already making his way left, taking care not to disturb anything on the tables.

"I think I see them," he said. "Don't touch anything if you can help it. I imagine that there are a good number of enchanted objects in here."

Vesper bit her lip and stayed put, watching as he stopped at a table that held racks upon racks of glass test tubes, each corked and labeled.

"What's in the rest of the tubes?" she wondered.

"Most anything you can think of," Kirael said, bending down to examine the labels. "Here we go..."

He extracted three narrow test tubes, each of which held a much smaller glass vial within.

"And hey..." Kirael reached into a flimsy cardboard box and held up two crosses. "Darren's prepared for anything, apparently."

Vesper smiled, but then paused. She turned toward the door. "Did you hear that?"

"What?" Kirael asked.

"Shhhhh..." she said, holding up a hand.

It took a moment, but then it came again. A very soft sound, like a mouse nibbling in the walls. Faint, but definitely not a figment of her imagination.

"I think we might have company," she said.

The sound got louder and louder, making Vesper's heart pound. After half a minute, it sounded almost like people were standing all around the room, pounding on the walls in a soft, insistent beat.

"What the Hell is that?" Vesper asked, swallowing.

"I don't want to find out," Kirael said. He stuck his hands out, palms face up, balancing the glass vials on one and the crosses on the other. Closing his eyes, he vanished them from sight.

"Nice trick. Don't suppose you can do that to us, can you? I don't think we're going back through that door..." Vesper said, pointing.

The door started to glow a little, throwing strange shadows through the room.

"Suppose not," Kirael said.

He worked his way over to the closest window, prying at the sash. Though he visibly struggled to raise it, he managed to open it fully.

"We can't just jump!" Vesper protested. "You'd be fine, but I'd break all my bones."

"We aren't going to jump," Kirael said, cocking his head. "Or rather, we are going to jump, but we're not going to fall."

Vesper stared at him, wondering if he'd lost his mind. "Sorry?"

"I'm an angel, Vesper. I can fly."

She felt her mouth form a surprised oh, then blushed.

"Right. I mean, of course you can. It's just..." she hesitated.

"I can't exactly walk around with my wings out, can I?" Kirael said, glancing at the door. "Now come on, we're running out of time."

Sucking in a breath, Vesper inched her way around the tables. Kirael climbed onto the window sill and stuck his head out, then stood up. Vesper quailed, watching him hold onto the window with one hand.

"Vesper, come on. This is not the time to lose your edge," Kirael said. "Just sit on the windowsill and I'll carry you, okay?"

"Right. Okay," she said, blowing out the breath she'd been holding. She squeezed out the window, trying not to let fear rule her thoughts.

Behind her, she heard the door splinter and fall; someone was coming for them, right on their heels.

Then she shrieked, because Kirael jumped off the house, dropping like a stone for a few seconds. Her shriek died in her throat, because the most amazing thing happened: she saw his wings for the first time.

Exploding like twin lightning bolts, his wings unfurled from his back, so beautiful they were unbelievable. Each wing was bigger than Kirael himself, a graceful arch of brilliant white feathers.

"Vesper!" Kirael said, and she could sense that someone was right behind her. "Jump!"

There was no more time to hesitate. She was just going to have to trust that Kirael wouldn't let her fall.

Letting her eyes close, Vesper pushed off the house, wincing as she dropped. That dizzying, gut-wrenching sensation of freefall.

Then, like magic, she stopped short. Strong arms caught her; she opened her eyes to find Kirael cradling her against his chest.

For an electric second, their gazes caught and held. A thousand things were just on the tip of Vesper's tongue, but she couldn't manage any of them.

"Hold on," he said, his lips twitching with sudden humor.

She felt Kirael's body ripple as he flapped both of his wings, a mighty push that shot them skyward. Vesper made a sound, half terror and half glee, and the world fell away beneath them.

"Can I..." she asked, looking up at his wings. "Can I touch?"

Kirael glanced down at her for a moment, his brow hunching. "Maybe later. My wings are very sensitive to touch. It would be... distracting."

The tone of his voice made her even more curious, but she held her tongue. She watched him as he worked. He was all effortless power as he carried them off into the night, his stunningly white wings outlined against the darkened sky.

Growing overwhelmed, she closed her eyes and rested her cheek against Kirael's neck. Sucking in a big lungful of his scent, she tried not to sigh like a smitten school girl.

Enjoy the moment for what it is, don't look for more than that, she told herself.

After all, how many chances would she get to be carried off into the sunset by a Fallen angel?

14

KIRAEL

Flying with Vesper in his arms was a strange experience for Kirael. On one hand, all he could think about was how incredibly fragile she was, how if anything happened, if he made a single mistake, it would be fatal.

On the other hand, despite the fact he was fairly certain that some of Darren's mages were tracking them across the city, Kirael was enjoying the moment. It was perverse, but feeling Vesper's soft curves pressed against him, the calm and trusting look on her face...

For the first time in memory, Kirael was glad that he was Fallen. Angels were awe-inspiring creatures, but their rigid purity of being kept them from many things. Everything was very black and white for them, nothing in between.

Complex emotions, like the guilty pleasure Kirael felt as he held Vesper close... angels couldn't experience that. Nor did they have enough empathy to truly engage with humans.

Especially humans as perplexing as Vesper. Tough as nails, but willing to lay down her life and literally walk into Hell for her sister. Beautiful, but utterly uninterested in her own looks. Brave, even in the face of deep-seated doubts.

Then there was the effect she had on Kirael... it seemed that, of late, every single time he saw her he felt...

Well, he *longed*. That was a feeling he'd never experienced for a person — the only real longing he'd ever felt was his desire to return to Heaven, to undo the damage he'd wrought.

If he were feeling especially honest, he might be able to admit that the sense of longing he felt for Heaven was mostly regret, mixed with an unspeakable guilt.

When he looked at Vesper, his longing was... complicated. His body tensed when he got a whiff of her scent. His stomach turned over when she gave him one of her rare smiles. She'd been on his mind the last few days, without a doubt.

She was unique; perhaps that was the sum of his restless curiosity.

Still, he didn't hesitate to take his time losing their pursuers, spend a little longer with Vesper in his arms. At some point, she seemed to lapse into sleep, or at least grow quiet and still.

He took her up as far as her need for oxygen allowed, flew her way out toward the Louisiana coast before spiraling back in towards New Orleans.

He told himself that he was just being cautious, that a few extra wide circles around the city would be prudent.

Nothing more than that. He was Fallen, she was a highly independent human with a messy, busy life. There could be no more than that, except perhaps the most occasional moments of friendship.

Fool, a voice in his head sounded. *This is a path you cannot travel.*

Pushing the whole matter from his thoughts, Kirael slowly descended toward the French Quarter. Vesper stirred moments before he touched down in the alley beside his house.

He tucked his wings in, sadly vanishing them.

Vesper stretched and blinked at the place where his wings

were before, then stared up at him for a few moments. "We're back?"

"That we are."

Kirael set her on her feet, steadying her when she wobbled for a moment. She made a frustrated sound.

"I think my right foot fell asleep," she said, shaking her bare foot.

"Will you live?" Kirael asked. The joke slipped from his mouth before he thought better of it, surprising them both.

"I..." Vesper said, then laughed. "Yes, I guess I will."

She moved toward the main street, clearly trying to determine their location.

"We're next to my place," Kirael said, nodding toward his apartment. "Darren sent some of his people to follow us. I'm fairly sure I lost them, but... it probably wouldn't hurt to lay low here for a while."

"Oh yeah?" she said, arching a brow.

"Unless your apartment is also warded with a spell of secrecy," Kirael said, suppressing the urge to roll his eyes. "Must you make everything difficult?"

A strange look flashed on Vesper's face, something close to hurt. "No. I'm just trying to be practical."

"Come on, then," Kirael said, walking over to the side entrance of his apartment. "If you'll lend me your keys, I'll have someone go pick up some clothes and things for you."

"No! No," Vesper said, shaking her head. "I'll have my coworker drop some stuff off."

He pressed his fingertips against a flat black electronic screen to the left of the door. After a moment, a buzzer sounded and the door opened with a mechanical whirr.

"Fancy," he heard Vesper mutter as he opened the door and motioned her inside.

"Not my doing," he said with a shrug. "After you."

He followed her up the two flights of stairs, then opened

the second security door by typing a ten-digit numerical passcode into another electronic pad.

Once they stepped into his apartment, Kirael realized his mistake. There was nothing to *do* in his apartment. He had a two bedrooms, two bathrooms, a kitchen, living room, and personal gym. Plenty for him, but...

He'd never entertained a guest here before, unless he counted Mere Marie's random appearances. In fact, the moment he brought Vesper here before was the first time he'd ever allowed *anyone* in his home.

Vesper didn't notice his discomfort, making her way into his kitchen without a moment's hesitation.

"Where are the glasses?" she asked, opening a cabinet at random.

"Left of the sink," he said.

Vesper poured herself a glass of water, then took a long drink. Turning to face him, she leaned against his kitchen counter. "Now what?"

"That wasn't enough excitement for you?" he asked, amused.

"I didn't ask you to juggle," she fired back, but he noticed a sparkle of humor in her eyes. "I meant that we should sit down and plot out our next few moves, get ahead of the curve."

"Tomorrow," he said with a shrug. "Tonight, I plan to have a glass of expensive whisky and then rest."

Maybe two glasses of whisky, to make sure he didn't toss and turn and try to suss out the mystery of Vesper tonight.

"That actually sounds pretty good," she said, finishing her water and returning to the sink for a second glass.

"Right this way," he said, leading her into the living room.

Vesper dropped onto one end of the couch. Kirael felt her eyes on his back as he moved to the side board where he kept his small stash of fine whiskeys, pouring two glasses.

When he handed her a glass, she set her water aside and

rose, taking a sip. For a long moment, there was palpable tension in the air.

Another first; Kirael couldn't remember ever feeling *awkward* around someone before.

Vesper walked over to examine the two racks of DVDs that hung on the wall beside his flat screen TV. After a second, she made an amused sound.

"The Dresden Files, huh?" she asked.

"Are you a fan?" he asked, taking a seat on the couch.

"I like the show," she said with a shrug. "Since he's sort of supposed to be in our world, it feels a little silly." She paused, "Then again, I watch Buffy, so…"

"I don't know what that is," he said.

Her immediate look of horror almost made him laugh out loud.

"You've never seen Buffy the Vampire Slayer?" she asked, like he'd just admitted to killing puppies for fun.

"I have not."

"Oh man," she said, giving her head a disbelieving shake. "Do you have Netflix?"

"I don't know."

"Where's the remote?" she asked, growing impatient.

Retrieving it from the table beside him, he handed it over. Vesper had the whole thing set up in very short order, explaining the whole thing to him. Most of it went over his head, but he didn't mind.

Her excitement was entertaining. She started the show, even going so far as to turn off the lights. Vesper sat beside him on the couch, launching into a detailed explanation of the show and the characters.

"And that's Spike… he's my favorite, such a badass…" she said. Kirael wondered if she realized that she had a huge smile pasted on her face.

After a full episode, Kirael had to admit he liked it, though he couldn't match Vesper's excitement.

"It's basically amazing," she said, beaming.

"It's not very surprising that you like it," he said. "Seeing as you're kind of the real-life version of her, right?"

Vesper's expression turned to sheer astonishment, her mouth dropping open for a moment. "I... that's... really nice of you to say..."

Kirael had to laugh at that. "Well, different hair... but you both slay demons, don't you?"

"I don't slay them," she qualified. "But... yeah. I know it's dumb that I even like this show, since it's basically a TV show about my actual job. But there's a lot of interpersonal drama too."

"Yeah, and everyone is really attractive," he said with a wink.

Her cheeks went bright pink, which made Kirael's smile grow wider. She sipped her whisky and glanced away, setting it on the coffee table.

Then as he watched, Vesper sucked in a breath, tipping her head back and looking up at him with wide eyes. Her gaze dropped to his lips for a moment, then she moved to press her lips to his.

Kirael struggled not to growl low in his chest. She was all heat and sweetness, her lips soft and inviting. She leaned into him, her lush breasts brushing his chest, one small hand coming up to cup the back of his neck.

Kirael couldn't resist the siren's call of her touch. He buried one hand in her hair, his thumb under her jaw to control the angle of the kiss.

He teased her lips with his tongue and she opened for him. He took his time, teasing and nipping, until she moaned into his mouth.

Fallen were no strangers to seduction, by any means. Kirael knew exactly how to draw a woman into his bed, had a calculated strategy for times when seduction might be necessary for a mission, or to appease his own boredom.

Usually by now he'd be formulating every single step in his head, anticipating, pushing the whole thing forward as quickly as possible.

With Vesper, though, it all fell away.

There was just *her*. Her taste, the soft sounds she made. The way she inched closer and closer. The feel of her fingers tugging gently at his hair, just at the nape of his neck.

He wanted to bend her back on the couch, strip off her dress, taste her exquisite skin. He wanted her on top, breasts bouncing as she rode him until she came, shouting his name.

He didn't wonder if she would be good. He *knew* she would be everything he could want, that she would probably blow his mind.

And yet... though he could have taken things further, likely even taken her to bed, gotten her out of his system and off his mind...

He didn't. He kept the kiss hot but controlled. Cupped her breast over her shirt, just to hear the sharp intake of her breath, just to know that she wanted him.

This will have to be enough, he told himself. *You are on a mission. You have nothing to offer her. Taking it any further would be the ultimate act of selfishness.*

When Vesper lifted the hem of his shirt, her warm fingers exploring his hip, he broke the kiss. Sighing, he leaned his forehead against hers for a beat, eyes closed.

"I have nothing to give you, Vesper," he said. He wanted to say more, to explain himself, but he lacked the words.

"I—" she started, then stopped. She pulled away from him, shaking off his touch. "Okay."

"I have a guest bedroom," he said.

Her gaze narrowed for a second, then she shrugged. "Fine."

"I have some things to do, so I'll just show you where it is," he said, clearing his throat.

His second experience with awkwardness bloomed, the tension in the air thick enough to cut with a knife.

He stood, turning the TV off, and walked her to the guest room. After a brief explanation of where she could find towels for the guest bathroom, he left to dig up a shirt for her to sleep in.

When he brought it to her, she gave him a glassy look.

"Thanks," she said, then shut the bedroom door in his face.

I suppose I deserved that, he thought.

Heading back to the living room, he picked up both the empty whisky glasses and carried them to the kitchen. He rinsed them and put them in the dishwasher, his mind turning over and over the same thoughts.

What is this pull I feel toward Vesper?

And, *does she feel the connection, or just physical desire?*

And, *why in the name of Lucifer am I this concerned about what anyone thinks?*

Then, *she's just a human woman.*

And, *so why can't I stop thinking about her?*

Growing tired of the cycle, Kirael went to his bedroom and changed into gym shorts, then headed to his miniature gym. It just had a treadmill, free weights, a heavy bag, and some other small equipment, but it was his escape.

He went at the punching bag for a good fifteen minutes, working out a little of his pent-up aggression. Then some weights, to stick with his usual routine.

Finally, he jumped rope for twenty minutes and hit the treadmill for thirty, running until he was about to fall down.

When Kirael finally showered and sought his bed, he felt a strange combination of exhaustion and restlessness. He closed his eyes, desperate now for sleep, but still he felt...

Unsettled. Unfinished.

Unsatisfied.

Rolling over and covering his face with a pillow, he groaned.

If he'd thought his fascination with Vesper dangerous before, now it was doubly so. He absolutely could not afford this distraction, not when he had too far to travel on his road to redemption.

Not only that, but getting involved with Vesper would be wrong. She might be every bit as amazing as her hero Buffy, but she had no real idea just how bad Kirael's past was…

If she'd flinched at his admission of being an assassin, she'd certainly turn tail and run if she heard a fraction of the things he *truly* regretted doing. Kirael was as bad as one of Buffy's villains, and his attempts at penitence didn't change that one bit.

Tossing the covers back, he crept back into the hallway. Feeling ridiculous, he put his ear to her door, listening.

Nothing.

Opening the door the barest inch, he listened again. All he could hear was her light, even breathing. Pushing it open further, he poked his head in.

Vesper was curled up on her side, covers drawn all the way up to her chin. He stood there, watching her, for longer than he'd like to admit.

It soothed him somehow, hearing the gentle sound of her breathing, seeing the subtle rise and fall of her body as she slept.

After a while, the cycle of anxious thoughts slowed, then stopped.

Then, and only then, did he silently close the door and return to his own room. The second he slid between the sheets, his head hitting the pillow, he was asleep.

He let the darkness pull him down, Vesper's face already floating through his dreams.

15

VESPER

"Morning."

Vesper looked up to find Kirael in the living room doorway, sipping a steaming mug of coffee. He was barefoot, wearing sweats and a t-shirt. His hair was still damp from the shower, curling at his nape.

"Hey," Vesper said, clearing her throat and dropping her gaze.

No need to stare, she chided herself. *After all, he's made his position perfectly clear.*

"Doing a little light reading?" he asked, lifting his chin to indicate the heavy book she held.

"Ah, yeah. You know what they say," she said. "Tolstoy's Anna Karenina always lifts the spirits, right?"

Kirael snorted. "Sure, if you're cheered by remorseless and unrepentant selfishness, and don't mind that there's not an ounce of redemption to be had. Not a world I want to live in."

Vesper set the book aside, glad that things between them weren't awkward. After the way they'd left things the night before, there was every possibility that this morning's conversation could have been uncomfortable, to say the least.

"I would've thought an angel got up a little earlier," she

said, checking the time on her cell phone. "It's nearly night again."

"Actually, I got up at nine this morning and went out to work. I'm just getting in from patrol."

"Patrol?" Vesper asked, curious.

"Just keep the peace in the city, make sure Kith are staying low key, make sure demons aren't taking over, and so forth. It's part of my agreement with Mere Marie."

"Ohhhhh, I get it. The Sainted Sinners are the new Alpha Guardians, huh?"

"I loathe that name," Kirael said, draining the remainder of his mug.

"Again, your taste is questionable. Is there more coffee?" she asked.

"There is, but you'll need to take it to go," Kirael said.

"You don't even have real clothes on," Vesper pointed out.

"Yeah, but I will soon. Make your coffee, get your boots on, and we can go."

"Go where?" she asked, but Kirael had already vanished into his bedroom.

When he returned, motorcycle helmet in hand, Vesper gave him an uncertain look.

"We could just take a cab," she suggested.

Kirael hesitated for a second, then shook his head. "Not for this."

"And what, pray, might that be?"

"We're going to see Stella," Kirael said, thrusting the helmet into Vesper's hands. "Come on, we need to get moving. No one misses an appointment with Stella."

"Are you gonna tell me who the Hell Stella is?" Vesper complained as she followed Kirael downstairs.

"Well... it's a long story. Not really mine to tell. But let's just say Stella is Lucifer's only surviving daughter."

Vesper gaped at him. "His *what*??"

Kirael gave her a pointed look, leading her to where his bike was parked.

"I just... I didn't think angels could procreate," Vesper said, astounded.

"It's not the easiest thing," Kirael said with a shrug. "And I'm not an angel."

"Kirael..." she said, grabbing his wrist and pulling him to a stop. "You are what you are. A single decision, one moment in time, is all that sent you chasing after Lucifer during the Fall. I don't think an angel ever stops being an angel."

Surprise flickered across his face, then his expression went stormy.

"I don't want to talk about this with you," he growled. "Now put the damn helmet on."

Blowing out a breath, Vesper did as she was told. Kirael climbed onto his bike, then beckoned for her to follow. She flung her leg over and slid her body down against his.

She slipped her arms around his waist, trying not to tense up as Kirael started the bike and took off.

The ride gave her a few quiet minutes to gather her thoughts.

While Kirael was out patrolling all day, Vesper had taken the liberty of calling up Vargus and asking for some details on Kirael. Vargus didn't find a whole lot in the couple of hours allotted, but two facts he dug up stuck out to Vesper.

One, Kirael was one of the very first creations. Meaning, before the Fall he served Heaven for untold millennia. Two, Kirael essentially did the same job in Heaven as he did in Hell — angel of vengeance, divine punisher of the unrepentant... assassin.

It made her insanely curious why he chose to Fall at all... To Vesper's thinking, it was essentially just a transfer from one place to another, with the added bonus of everlasting hellfire and guilt.

She couldn't help but wonder about the root of Kirael's insistence that he was no longer an angel.

Was it because he chose to Fall? Because he wanted to leave Heaven?

Kirael might be many things, but he was also moral. His own version of morality, anyway.

And yeah, maybe he was once a wet worker. Maybe he had a lot of deaths on his conscience. But Vesper was willing to bet her right hand that he'd never done so needlessly, or for personal reasons.

Her inference, from knowing him only this short while, was thus: Kirael was loyal to his cause, as long as the cause was worthy.

Losing faith in light of Lucifer's wrongdoing seemed like a no-brainer. But walking away from Heaven?

What could Kirael's reasoning for that possibly be? she thought.

Kirael pulled the bike to a stop in front of the Columns Hotel on St. Charles. The grand white antebellum mansion held a high-end cocktail lounge and restaurant downstairs; Vesper had driven by the place, but never actually gone in herself.

She got off the bike and handed over the helmet, staring up at the hotel.

"This is where Stella hangs out?" she asked, skeptical.

"She doesn't spend much time up here. Lucifer keeps a very close eye on Stella, with good reason. But yes, she does favor the Victorian Lounge."

"Hmm," Vesper said, reaching out to pluck at a piece of lint on Kirael's white Henley shirt.

He caught her hand with his, trapping it against his chest. For the briefest moment, their gazes caught. Vesper's heartbeat thrummed, a wild feeling surging inside her.

Then, slowly and deliberately, she pulled her fingers from his grasp and turned away. She heard Kirael clear his throat, but she didn't look back, didn't try to catch whatever expression was on his face, no matter how much she wanted to.

Vesper propelled herself up to the Hotel, taking the steps two at a time until she walked into the Hotel's foyer.

"I'm meeting someone in the Victorian Lounge," she told the concierge.

"Name?" he asked, barely looking up from the huge guest book spread on the podium before him.

"Lesange," Kirael said, right on Vesper's heels. He stopped right behind her, so close she could feel the heat radiating from his big body.

She shivered, but already the concierge was beckoning, leading them into the Lounge. Vesper slowed as they stepped inside the dark-paneled room.

"Wow, I am so underdressed," she said with a whistle.

"Don't worry about it," Kirael said, putting a hand on her lower back and urging her forward. "Keep moving, we're very close to being late."

The concierge showed them to a circular brown leather booth, where Lucan awaited. And next to him...

Could only be Stella.

Her hourglass curves were encased in a tight black sheath dress, showing plenty of cleavage and thigh. Her hair fell in rivers of white-gold waves, thick and long and shiny. Her lips were lacquered red as blood, and the perfection her enormous blue eyes and high cheekbones would've made Barbie jealous.

She and Lucan sat on one side of the booth, Lucan looking positively murderous while Stella smirked.

"We are not talking about this," Lucan growled, making Stella's eyes sparkle.

The relief on Lucan's face when he saw Kirael and Vesper approaching was almost comical.

"There you are," Lucan said, giving Kirael a questioning look.

"I was almost hoping you'd be late," Stella sighed. "Then it wouldn't be a double date."

Her voice made Vesper shiver; the blonde's voice was like the pealing of a high, clear bell. Kirael slid into the booth beside Stella, Vesper after him.

"This is not a *date*," Lucan said flatly, looking annoyed.

"Do you want my help, or not?" Stella said, crossing her arms.

Silence for a few minutes, and then Lucan shrugged. "Yes."

Vesper stared at Stella, trying to determine whether her beauty was real or the result of lots of cosmetics and surgery. When Stella turned the full force of her attention onto Vesper, Vesper nearly shrank back.

"Hmmm. You're a pretty one, aren't you?" Stella mused. "Ever thought of working for the Legion? My father is a very good employer, you'd have everything you ever wanted."

Vesper's mouth went dry, but she sat up a little straighter. "No."

"Pity," Stella said. "If you ever change your mind... well, I'll be listening."

"Is that a threat?" Vesper asked with a frown.

Kirael put his hand on her knee under the table, squeezing gently.

Stella canted her head, her gaze narrowing. "I don't make threats. I don't need to."

"Stella," Kirael cut in. "What is it that you need from us? We want to make our play as soon as possible."

Stella gave Vesper another moment's examination, then turned to Kirael.

"I just wanted to know why you'd take such a risk. I thought it might be the girl, but then I second-guessed myself. Could the high and mighty Kirael actually have some affection for a human?" she asked, a haughty smirk on her lips.

Kirael was silent a beat, staring at Stella. Vesper suddenly realized that Kirael couldn't tell Stella about the Null; Stella would certainly want Aurora for herself.

"Interesting," Stella said. "So this is what the Fallen get up to on Earth. Fraternizing with humans.... Lucan, darling, you'd better not get any ideas from your friend here."

She reached up to brush a lock of Lucan's ash blond hair back from his face. He flinched, pulling away from her, and for a moment Vesper saw a flash of anger and pain in Stella's expression.

"There's only one thing left, then," Stella said. "Lucan just has to agree to his end of this little bargain."

Everyone looked at Lucan, who looked a little ill.

"Fine, yes," he said. "I accept."

"Excellent," Stella purred. "I think we're done here."

She started to shoo Lucan out of her way.

"Wait..." Vesper started, but Kirael squeezed her knee hard.

"Yes?" Stella asked, arching a slender brow.

"Um... thank you. That's all," Vesper said, fidgeting.

Stella stared at her for a few seconds, then nodded and turned to Lucan. "I need seventy-two hours to put things in place. Madam White's, midnight. Don't be late. Now *move*."

Watching Lucan, perhaps the most powerful being Vesper had ever encountered, scramble to get out of Stella's way...

Interesting, Vesper thought. It certainly begged the question: *what's big and bad enough to make the Fallen afraid?* Lucifer's daughter, apparently.

Without a backward glance, Stella rose and strode out of the bar, hips swaying. People stopped mid-sentence and mid-sip to stare at her as she went, her four-inch heels clicking neatly on the wood floor.

"Wow," Vesper said, shaking her head as she and Kirael got out of the booth. "She's something else."

"You have no idea," Lucan murmured, still looking after Stella, though she was long gone. "'What, man, defy the devil.'"

Vesper looked to Kirael, who shrugged and said, "Shakespeare, I think."

"What's the deal there?" Vesper asked, nodding at Lucan.

Kirael just shook his head and changed the subject. "We should probably order Lucan a bottle of whisky and leave him to it."

Vesper laughed. Her jaw dropped a little when Kirael walked over to the bar, pulled out his wallet, and handed the bartender two 100s. After clapping Lucan on the back, Kirael shooed Vesper outside.

"Where are we going?" she asked.

Kirael looked thoughtful.

"I could eat."

"How about beignets? I could use some coffee and sugar."

"Been-yay?" he asked.

"Yeah, *beignet*. A French doughnut, I guess?"

"I'm not really sure how I feel about beignets."

"Uh... fried dough covered with a mound of powdered sugar? Is there any option other than '*Fuck Yes*'?"

Kirael smiled and handed over the helmet. "You know the drill."

He turned onto Royal Street and parked near his apartment.

"Thought we could walk," he said.

"It's nice weather for it," she agreed.

They strolled past a few blocks of shops and galleries, Vesper slowing to peer in a particular window.

"Keil's," she said, nodding at the sign. "My favorite antiques store."

"I see that you're more interested in the giant diamond rings than the French settees," Kirael said.

Vesper shot him a dirty look. "A girl can dream, okay? Come here."

Kirael came over, looking a little bored, and Vesper had to work hard not to stamp her foot.

"Look," she said, pointing. "That ring right there? One of a kind, bright canary diamond, set with baguette sapphires. I tried it on once, just to see if they'd let me. The shopkeeper was nice, but I could tell she wanted to roll her eyes."

"Why?" Kirael asked.

Vesper gave him a funny look. "That ring is like... a million dollars. Literally. Some queen of Scotland owned it, I guess."

Kirael's brows rose. "This is one of those moments where I realize that for all my time on Earth, I still don't completely understand humans."

Vesper had to laugh at that. "Fine, don't marvel then. Some people have no taste."

"Enough looking, more moving," Kirael said mildly.

Fifteen minutes later, they walked into Cafe du Monde in the French Quarter. The place was little more than a walk-up window next to a huge patio covered by a green and white striped awning... but it was undeniably delicious, and utterly New Orleans.

"Ooh, a table," she said, grabbing the last one in the corner. "If I stake it out, will you get us beignets?"

"Cafe au Lait?" Kirael asked.

"The biggest one they have, chicory if they got it."

Vesper brushed a little powdered sugar off the patio chairs and sat down, staring out into the street. People were strolling up and down the street, drinking and laughing. A horse-mounted cop went by, then a clown on stilts casual as you please.

People gathered at the end of the block, watching a pink-feathered Mardi Gras Indian shimmy in time to the sound of a nearby brass band. Vesper often got lost in the everyday details of her life, forgetting how amazing her city could be.

The moon was coming up, nearly full now, and the weather was a gorgeous seventy-five degrees. Plus, a hot man was heading her way with a tray of doughnuts and coffee. Life didn't get a whole lot better than this.

Kirael set down the beignets and coffees, then returned the tray. When he came back, he pulled up his chair beside hers and sat down.

"Street theater," he mused, sipping his coffee.

"People-watching is one of my favorite things," Vesper admitted. "I'm pretty nosy by nature."

"You?" Kirael teased, arching a brow. "I'm shocked."

Vesper shot him a playful glare, then picked up a plate with a small mountain of powdered sugar atop a square doughnut. She took a huge bite, giggling as the sugar spread all over her mouth and nose.

"Mmmm," she sighed, her mouth still full. "'S good."

"I've never tried them," Kirael said, picking up his own plate.

"What?" Vesper asked, swallowing. "Seriously?"

"Yep."

"Well, no time like the present," Vesper said.

Kirael picked up the doughnut and bit into it, clearly struggling not to laugh. Then he made a strangled sound, a sort of shocked moan.

"This is *good*," he said.

"Duh," Vesper said, rolling her eyes. "There's a reason it's a classic."

"Mmmf," was his only response.

They ate in silence for a couple of minutes, watching people pass by, content to settle into their own thoughts.

"So, how would you rate your first beignet experience?" Vesper asked once they were finished.

"What's the scale?" Kirael asked.

"Let's say one to ten."

"Hmmm..." he said, pretending to consider it. "Eight?"

"A difficult customer, I see," Vesper said. "Well, if the powdered sugar on your face is any indication, you liked the doughnuts just fine."

Kirael chuckled and wiped at his mouth with the back of his hand. "Better?"

"Hah. Uh... not really. Come here," Vesper said, moving closer to banish a smudge of white from above his lips.

Her thumb brushed over his upper lip, and their gazes suddenly locked. She shivered, her tongue darting out to wet her own lips. Vesper felt a little silly, but she couldn't help her reaction.

Then Kirael took her hand, turning her palm up. Not taking his eyes off her for a second, he placed a slow, burning kiss against her palm, another over her pulse.

Vesper made a soft sound, her lips parting. At once, they leaned into each other, lips crashing together. In seconds Kirael's tongue was stroking Vesper's, hands wound in each other's hair, coffee all but forgotten.

For a few seconds, the world fell away from them, just as it had when Kirael carried her skyward in his arms. His taste was clean and masculine and heady, and Vesper lost herself in it.

A pigeon swooped down, wings flailing as it tried to land on the table and make off with the last bite of Kirael's beignet. Vesper and Kirael jumped apart, and Vesper laughed.

"Nice job, pigeon," she said to the bird as she waved it away from their table.

Kirael stood. "Listen, Vesper..."

Vesper looked up at him, then rolled her eyes.

"Don't," she warned him.

"It's not you—"

Vesper stood, feeling anger surge in her heart.

"Seriously? It's not like I keep pouncing on you," she snapped.

"I didn't say that."

"Well, you've said plenty."

She brushed the remaining powdered sugar off her dark jeans and then turned to leave.

"Where are you going?" Kirael asked.

"Not your concern. I'll see you on the full moon."

"Vesper, wait—"

She headed toward the street car, fuming. Out of the corner of her eye, she saw Kirael behind her. Whirling, she pointed an accusatory finger at him.

"Kirael, I fucking mean it. Do *not* follow me."

He raised both his hands in a sign of surrender. With one last glare, Vesper charged off in the opposite direction, desperate to get away from him.

Dumb, dumb move, she told herself. Don't you ever learn?

Picking up her pace, she wished she could abandon her self-doubt as easily as she'd left Kirael behind on the street...

16

KIRAEL

Kirael paced the street outside Vesper's apartment, occasionally pausing to look up at the black wrought-iron balcony that he estimated was hers. Two nights ago, he'd let her walk away, knowing her anger and frustration were not without merit.

He was going through a bit of a sea change, trying to adjust from old to new. Once, he'd been among Heaven's most exalted creations. Then he'd Fallen, becoming one of Lucifer's most prized bringers of death.

In both capacities, he'd been intensely dedicated to his cause. Even after growing disillusioned with his work in Hell, he'd still carried out his duties with a fierce loyalty.

In truth, he'd come to see Heaven and Hell as a sort of balancing cycle. Kirael saw it as being like the water cycle in the human world: rain falling to the ocean, then evaporating and rising to begin anew.

Heaven and Hell were like that, if you observed from a distance over several millennia. Souls came into the world, lived on Earth for a short time, and then went to Heaven or Hell. Eternity was a relative term; eventually a soul would fade from existence, its energy flowing into the creation of a new soul.

Or at least that was Kirael's theory. In truth, the process was unknowable. Still, Kirael had been a vital part of it, culling aging souls, making room for new ones.

He was necessary.

Here, on Earth? He was the same insignificant speck of dust as everyone else, and it felt...

Frightening. Not to mention that his future was up in the air. Unless Lucifer or Metatron struck him down, Kirael would live on and on. No Heaven, no Hell... just Earth.

Every time he saw Vesper, it just reminded him of all the new concepts he was struggling with. She drew him like a moth to a flame, but she was also human. Fleeting, fragile. A tender flower growing in a bed of thorns, danger blossoming all around her.

In the short time he'd known her, she'd protected herself admirably. But a single chance encounter with any of Kirael's former comrades, and Vesper would cease to *exist*.

Given that she had such a relatively short time on Earth, Kirael couldn't help but think that she deserved a lot more than the life she lived. She shouldn't be stuck hunting down demons in the dark, or endlessly trying to rescue her luckless sister.

And she sure as Hell shouldn't be making eyes at Kirael. She should be with someone who could give her what she needed; Kirael couldn't even begin to guess what that might be.

She should be with someone who didn't dream of all the people he killed. Someone whose soul wasn't soaked with the blood of a thousand kills. Or ten thousand... there was truly no counting at this point.

"What are you doing here?"

Kirael looked up to find Vesper approaching, her leather jacket slung over one shoulder, a grim look on her face.

"Waiting for you," he said.

She glanced up at her apartment, her brow knitting. "You shouldn't be here."

"I didn't like how we left things the other night. I wanted to explain—"

"No need," she said, cutting him off.

"I think there is."

"Kirael..." she said, crossing her arms, "You've made yourself clear. I promise you that."

"I just want you to know it's not your fault," he said.

Vesper rolled her eyes, "Please stop."

"It's complicated, is all I'm saying."

She glanced up toward her balcony again. Kirael thought he saw some movement inside.

"Do you have a roommate?" he asked, narrowing his gaze.

"Are we done here?" she asked, her tone sharp.

"No. I have more news."

Vesper crossed her arms and canted her head. "So?"

Holding out his right hand, palm up, he summoned a heavy set of iron keys. Holding them up for Vesper to see, he shook them gently.

"Fancy skeleton keys," she said, examining them. Each of six keys was long and thin, all different colors, each with a grinning skull at the end.

"The keys to Lucifer's private rooms."

He saw her relax a little, and she nodded. "Cool. How'd you get them?"

"Beat the tar out of a Shkisa demon."

Vesper's brows shot up. "I've never had the pleasure. I hear they're nasty."

"Yeah. Well, this one defected from Hell last month. Once I tracked him down, he had plenty to say."

"More than just the keys?"

"Yeah. A safe house, just a couple blocks from where your sister is being kept. He's going to arrange for it to be empty on the day we need it."

She pursed her lips, thoughtful. He was glad that her curiosity seemed to have taken some of the edge off her anger.

"How do you know we can trust him?" she asked.

Kirael blew out a breath. "I don't, but I think it's the best we can do."

"Okay. Well... thanks," she said after a moment.

Kirael scrubbed a hand through his hair. "I was hoping you'd come back to my place, work through the plan for tomorrow night."

She hesitated, then nodded. "Okay."

"Okay?" Kirael asked, surprised. "Just like that?"

"Just like that," she said. "If you can wait here for a couple minutes, let me grab some things from my apartment."

"No problem," Kirael said, feeling suspicious of her sudden compliance.

She gave him a long look, then blew out a breath. "Okay. Give me five minutes."

Vesper vanished into her building. Kirael sat on her steps, sprawling out to wait. He closed his eyes and took in a couple of deep breaths, reminding himself of his purpose.

Get The Book of Names. Find the Null. Prostrate yourself to Metatron, and hope for a positive response from Heaven. At the very least, prove the depth of your regrets...

His eyes snapped open. He found a sickly-looking young woman shuffling up to him. Her ratty jeans and tank top smelled of cigarettes, and she had dark circles under her eyes like twin smudges of midnight ink. Her glassy-eyed, slightly open-mouthed expression screamed *junkie*.

She was walking in a crooked path, but staring at Vesper's door with a singular kind of focus.

"Hey, hey," Kirael said, quick to his feet. "You need something?"

She halted and stared at him for a second. This close, he could see the bruises on her neck, her inner arms. She might be a drug user, but she was certainly regularly donating her blood to Vampyres. Straight from the vein, too.

"V-v-vesper," the woman wheezed. "V-vesper Emery."

She untucked a small white box from under her arm, waving it at Kirael.

"You're not going in there," he said. Crossing his arms and straightening his back, he wasn't a bit subtle about using his stature to emphasize his words.

"Vesper. Vesper Emery," she said again, blinking rapidly. He could see a little sweat break out on her brow, her pupils big and dark.

"Give it to me," he said, holding out a hand.

She stared at him again, calculating. "Vesper Emery?"

"Yes," he said.

"Vesper Emery," the woman said one last time, thrusting the box out at him. He took it; it was only a little bigger than his hand, maybe two inches thick. Like the gift box a necklace would come in, maybe. Light enough, though when he gave it a little shake he could hear a soft clink and thud.

The strangest part was that it was tied with a bright red ribbon. That part made his stomach churn.

"Okay. Go," he said, motioning for her to leave.

Another moment of blinking, then she turned and shambled off, disappearing around the corner.

Vesper swept out of her building, a black messenger bag wrapped around her torso.

"Ready?" she asked.

Kirael hesitated. "This was just delivered, supposedly for you."

"What? Did you send it?" she asked, her mouth pulling into a frown.

"No."

"Well, give it to me," she said as she stuck out her hand, immediately losing patience.

"I think I should open it," he said. "The messenger was... unusual."

Vesper crossed her arms. "I don't know what that means."

"I'm fairly sure that this is a delivery from the Vampyres," he said. "If I had to guess."

All the color drained from Vesper's face. "Shit."

"Yeah."

"Okay. So open it," she said, biting her lip.

Kirael stepped away from her, untying the bow and pulling off the lid. He froze.

"Shit," he murmured.

"What is it?" Vesper demanded. "Is it dangerous? Let me see."

There was nothing in the world that Kirael wanted less than to show her, but of course he had no choice. He tilted the box so that she could see.

Two thin glass vials, nestled in a piece of white silk. Each one held a bit of red liquid. Next to the vials was a small card. Printed on the card was: Drisgell House — Sample — Mercedes. At the bottom of the card there was a little arrow scrawled, indicating that the card should be turned over.

Vesper made a strangled sound, her hand flying to her mouth.

Feeling heartsick, Kirael turned the card over. Written on the back was a note: *there's more where this comes from... but how much more?*

They'd sent her Mercy's *blood*.

"Ohhhh..." Vesper said, wobbling.

Kirael moved to try to steady her, but she shrieked and jumped back.

"Get that *away* from me!" she said, turning green.

"Right..." Kirael said. "Should I throw it away?"

"God, yes," Vesper said, pressing the heels of her hands against her eyes. "Just get rid of it, please."

Kirael disposed of the box in a nearby trashcan, then returned to Vesper.

"Come on, let's walk. I don't like the idea of the Vampyres knowing where you are," he said.

Vesper dropped her hands, giving him a mournful look.

"Kirael... they're going to kill her," she whispered, her voice breaking.

"No, no..." he said, wrapping an arm around her. "Come on."

Vesper didn't cry, didn't say anything else at all as he escorted her to his apartment. Once they were safely inside again, he settled her on the couch.

"Coffee? Or tea?" he asked, crouching down before her and taking her hands.

"Liquor," she said.

"We've got too much to do tonight. The planning is more important than ever," he said, trying to keep his tone gentle.

Vesper looked up from her lap, her eyes shining with unshed tears. "Sit with me for a minute, then?"

Kirael moved to sit next to her on the couch. To his distinct surprise, Vesper leaned against him, pressing her face into his shoulder. He slid his arm around her shoulders, pulling her close.

She was so vulnerable, so yielding. This private, soft side of Vesper was devastating to Kirael, making him yearn for her in ways he'd never experienced before.

Unable to resist her allure, he buried his nose in her hair. She smelled of vanilla and spice, sweet and clean. He wanted to bury his hands in her hair, tip back her head, kiss her lips until her sorrows melted away.

When Vesper pulled back, looking up at him with those big ocean-blue eyes, Kirael groaned aloud. He cupped her cheek, and she covered his hand with her own, her eyes searching his face.

"Kirael..." she whispered.

"Damn me," he whispered back, a moment before he kissed her.

His lips found hers, ravenous and hot. The mere touch of her tongue set him aflame, and the way she opened for him made him burn higher and higher. Kirael grabbed her by the waist and dragged Vesper onto his lap, straddling him, giving her the control for a moment.

She tossed back the dark curtain of her hair with a sigh, digging her fingers into his hair, kissing him fiercely. Her hips rocked gently against his, her breasts brushing his chest.

"You're so beautiful," he murmured against her lips.

Vesper grasped one of his hands and dragged it up to cup her full breast through her shirt, then gasped when Kirael brushed his thumb across her nipple.

"Yes," she whispered, urging him on.

In a matter of seconds, Kirael had her shirt pushed up to her shoulders, pulling down the cups of her bra to expose her gorgeous breasts. Perfectly lush and round, with puckered pink nipples that he couldn't help but explore with his tongue. He shaped both her breasts in his hands, tasting them greedily, the sound of Vesper's soft cries pushing him on and on.

When she shifted to kiss him again, his hands drifted down to her hips, gripping them to press her harder against his growing erection. The friction of her warm heat against him, even through their jeans, was absolutely killing him.

"I want you," Vesper whispered, rolling her hips in time with Kirael's.

He couldn't stop thinking about how amazing it would be to take her, to fill her, have her ride him just like this. She'd be so hot and tight, crying his name as he made her come over and over...

"Am I intruding?" came a loud voice from the hallway.

Kirael and Vesper both froze, Vesper quickly pulling her shirt down. They both turned at once.

Mere Marie stood in the doorway of the living room, arms crossed, a terribly sour expression on her face.

"All my charges, like a bunch of horny teenaged boys," Mere Marie spat.

"Ummm..." Vesper said, sliding off Kirael's lap. Her face was ten shades of red, and Kirael felt a little embarrassed himself.

"Why are you here?" Kirael asked, clearing his throat as he stood and adjusted himself, not trying to hide anything.

"I came to help you plan for your little break-in," Mere Marie said. "You called me three hours ago, remember?"

That much was certainly true. Kirael glanced at Vesper, who couldn't seem to meet his gaze.

"I'll give you two a moment," Mere Marie said, intentionally making things more awkward.

"No, no," Vesper said, standing up as she righted her clothing. "This was a mistake, that's all."

Mere Marie's arched brows indicated that she agreed.

"Let's get down to business, then," she said. "By business, I mean the business of saving your sister."

Scowling, Kirael watched as Mere Marie swept in with a stack of books and notes, ready to tackle their planning session head on.

Maybe it's better that she interrupted, he thought. Still it didn't stop him from feeling strangely wistful and bitter.

Or from staring at Vesper, longing for her touch...

17

KIRAEL

Kirael stood on a hill, looking down as the first fiery rays of morning began to illuminate the battle field. His sword was heavy in his hand, but it was no comfort to him.

Belial walked up beside him, adjusting his leather armor. He smelled of liquor, mixed with the faint musk of the whore he'd lain with the night before. Tall, dark, and classically handsome, Belial never denied himself the pleasures of the human world.

Kirael could barely stand to look at him, the Fallen he'd fought beside since time immemorial.

Far across the dusty expanse, human fighters straggled into sight, their white turbans bright against the rubble-strewn ground. åAll around them, the bombed-out remnants of the city lay like fallen soldiers.

"You look like shit," Belial said, holding out his hand to summon his sword.

Kirael glanced at him, but didn't respond. Though they'd done this countless times, descending on an impending battle and wreaking havoc to ensure their outcome, this time felt...

Different.

"This is wrong," Kirael said at length. "These men will be defenseless against us."

"I can see their guns from here," Belial grunted.

"You know what I mean," Kirael said. "We'll slaughter them. It will be a bloodbath."

"That's rich, coming from you."

Kirael scowled. "We are not needed here."

"And yet, Lucifer commanded us to settle this fight. What more do you need?"

"Angels battling humans," Kirael spat. "It is unjust."

Belial turned to him, his expression hard. "What is your problem?"

Kirael was quiet for a beat.

"Do you never tire of it?"

"Of battle? Never."

"Of bringing death," Kirael corrected him. "Do you never wish for more? In the beginning, before the Fall, we all swore to bring a new world order."

"And we have. We've influenced every major event in the history of humanity," Belial said.

"We were going to bring back the Garden," Kirael continued, ignoring him. "We were going to raise humans up, end their suffering. Now, we only kill."

"It is our designation, it's what we were designed to do," Belial said, shaking his head. "For there to be life, there must be death."

"Our cause was lost, from the moment of the Fall. Now all we represent is trickery and deceit. Pain, mourning, death. We are only here to inflame the passions of these people, so that they will strike at their foes without thinking. This is beneath us, Belial."

Belial lifted his sword, considering it for a moment.

"You are close to treason, my friend," Belial said.

Kirael's heart dropped. "I only want what Lucifer promised, in the beginning—"

Belial whirled on him. "Enough! We have everything that Lucifer sees fit to give us. Money, women, every luxury. It is a good life, if you will only accept it."

"Belial…"

"Not another word," the Fallen snapped. "Or I will cut your tongue from your mouth, shear your wings from your shoulders. I will take your head, if I can."

Kirael and Belial stared at one another for several long moments, breathing hard. After a moment, Belial stepped back.

"You need a break. After today, take some time to reflect. Even the most loyal heart tires after so much time, Kirael. I know you, friend. I know you do not intend treason."

Kirael dropped his gaze. He wasn't sure what he meant, not anymore.

Belial clapped him on the shoulder. "Prepare yourself for the fight. After this, we can discuss your thoughts in more depth."

Kirael let Belial's words soothe him, though part of him knew that discussion would not be enough.

"Hail Lucifer!" Belial said, raising his sword toward the battle field.

Enemy soldiers rushed toward them now, guns at the ready. Adrenaline filled Kirael's veins, and he too raised his sword.

As one, he and Belial cried out and rushed down into the thick of the battle, swords swinging. He raised his sword, ready to take his first life of the fresh dawn.

Before him, his first opponent rushed in, a boy of no more than seventeen. Gritting his teeth, Kirael plunged his sword down, straight through the soldier's chest.

As Kirael pulled his sword free, he watched the light in the boy's eyes flicker and fade. Suddenly, the boy's face shifted, his body shrinking.

The unknown boy morphed, and suddenly Vesper's body dropped to Kirael's feet. She gasped, blood pouring from her mouth. Her hands flew to the wound at the center of her chest, trying in vain to keep her life's blood from draining away...

"No!" Kirael shouted. "No!"

He blinked, and the battle field was gone. He stood in his own bedroom, naked and covered in sweat, shaking.

"No," he whispered, even though he knew it was only a dream.

He'd killed that boy, sure enough, and a hundred others on that day. And he regretted it to his core, as he now regretted every such act he'd committed in Lucifer's name.

"Vesper..." he said aloud, the sound of her name bitter on his lips.

This, this was the reason I can't... don't deserve...

He couldn't even finish the thought. Sitting on the edge of his bed, he dropped his head into his hands.

I am playing a dangerous game. This flirtation with Vesper... she needs a man whose hands are not wet with the blood of so many innocents...

And yet, as he forced himself to lie back down in his bed, he knew he would go to her. That he needed to see her, couldn't stay away. Even just to make sure she was safe. Even if he took nothing for himself...

That could be enough, couldn't it?

It will have to be enough.

18

VESPER

Vesper woke in the night, sitting up in bed. She glanced around Kirael's guest bedroom, her brain still fuzzy with sleep.

There, the sound came again. A low keening, sorrowful.

Kirael, she thought.

Rising, she threw back the blankets and padded out of her room. The wood floor was cold against her bare feet as she went to Kirael's bedroom door. It was open a crack, and she heard another groan.

Biting her lip and moving as quietly as possible, she nudged his door open wider.

"No!" he shouted suddenly, making her jump.

Vesper pushed the door wide. Moonlight splashed across his bed, illuminating Kirael as he slept. He was naked except for a slip of sheet around his hips, sprawled on his stomach.

He made another low sound, the muscles in his back rippling and tensing.

"Forgive me..." he whispered, his fists clenching. The broken plea tugged at Vesper's heart strings; she should wake him, free him from his nightmare.

Softly as she could, she moved close and put a hand on Kirael's shoulder.

"Kirael," she whispered. "Kirael, wake up."

He shifted onto his back, but didn't open his eyes.

"Kirael," she said, a little louder.

His eyes snapped open, unfocused. He sat up, grabbing her arm and yanking her down onto his lap. His breathing went harsh, and then he blinked at her.

"Vesper," he said, her name sounding melodic from his lips.

Vesper's breath caught in her chest as they stared at each other. Kirael's gaze dropped to her lips and her heartbeat sped to a gallop. When he leaned in to brush his lips over hers, she accepted him without a moment's thought.

The mere touch of their lips was like putting a match to flame. Suddenly, she couldn't get close enough to him. Suddenly, her panties and t-shirt were stifling; she wanted to feel Kirael's skin against her own, wanted to feel his heart beat in time with hers.

"Ah, Vesper..." he murmured, laying back on the bed.

He took her with him, laying her out atop his body. Letting Vesper feel every inch of his muscular body, feel his heavy erection pressed against her belly. No matter what he said, there was no doubt that he wanted her.

And Vesper was starving for him, burning alive with the need for his hands on her skin, his lips and tongue driving her wild. She was a person who tried not to need anyone, not to become dependent.

But at this moment, right here and now, she'd never needed anyone like she needed Kirael.

He tugged her shirt up over her head, baring her too-warm skin to the moonlight. His hands gripped her hips, skated up her ribs, shaped her breasts. He surged upward, his lips leaving her mouth to explore her neck, her collarbone, her already-aching nipple.

The wet heat of his mouth was almost more than she could

handle. Vesper cried out when his teeth scraped her sensitive flesh, her hips grinding against his in response.

"Kirael, yes," she moaned. "I need you..."

He froze for a moment, a low growl rattling in his chest. Then Kirael spread his big hands around her waist and flipped her onto her back, covering her with his big body. The sheet slipped away, leaving him naked, showing her exactly what Kirael offered.

His sheer perfection took her breath away.

Vesper was desperate to touch him, running a hand from his back down to his taut backside. Pure muscle, not an ounce wasted. Kirael took her lips once more, gently thrusting against her through her panties.

They kissed, breathing hard. Vesper explored the rigid vee of muscles at his hip, then shifted to put a little space between them. Just enough to trail her fingers down until she circled her fingers around his cock.

Her sound of surprise was involuntary. Long, thick, and hot as fire, the feel of him in her hand made heat pool low in her body. Images flashed in her mind, images of Vesper on her knees, trying to take all of him in her mouth. Images of Kirael taking her hard from behind, of the look on his face when he sank deep inside her for the first time.

"Yes," she moaned.

Kirael captured her hands, pulling them up over her head, and kissed her deeply. He pulled her panties off in a single smooth motion, raising her anticipation another notch.

He cupped her breast, slid his hand down to tease her hip, then trailed his touch down to her knee. He parted her thighs and she opened for him, feeling herself blush even as her breath caught.

The brush of a single fingertip against her wetness made her moan. His thumb found her clit, rubbing in slow circles, and Vesper thought she might die right then and there.

"You're so wet for me already," Kirael said, leaning down to kiss the hollow of her throat, the slope of her neck.

She shivered, reaching for him, pulling him closer. "Please, Kirael. Don't make me wait."

"Mmmm," he murmured, giving her another deep kiss on the lips. "Come here."

He rolled onto his back again, pulling her atop him so that she straddled him boldly. She gasped as her heat met the length of his cock, making her ache for him, ache to be stretched and filled completely.

"Take what you want, Vesper," Kirael growled, looking up at her with passion-darkened eyes.

Vesper bit her lip, grasping his cock and rising to settle against him. Throwing her head back, she moaned as she slid down onto him, taking him slow, inch by inch.

"You're so big," she said, working her hips to take his whole length.

Kirael gripped her hips and thrust up into her in one rough movement, making them both cry out.

"So good," Vesper moaned, setting a slow rhythm, rocking up and down.

He pulled her down for a kiss, cupped one of her breasts, and ran his hands all over her body.

"You're so beautiful," he said. "I've never wanted anyone so much."

Vesper moved faster, her heart thrumming. Kirael moved with her, keeping things quick and light.

"I want more," Vesper groaned. "Harder and deeper."

She gasped as Kirael flipped her onto her back, pressing one of her knees up to her chest while keeping the other leg flat against the bed. He began to fill her in quick, hard thrusts, making her entire body tense and tighten.

"Yes, yes," she whispered, raking her nails over his shoulders, his back. Rocking up to meet his every movement.

Kirael put a hand under her lower back, lifting her the

barest inch, but it was just enough to drive Vesper wild. He stroked in and out, hitting the same wonderful spot deep inside her, making her feel as though wildfire spread through her veins.

"Oh, oh, I'm going to..." she started, then shattered with a loud cry.

Pulsing and clenching tightly, Vesper clung to Kirael.

"Fuck, you're so good," he told her, moving his hands to her hips again, lifting her, his fingers digging into her flesh. "Vesper, *yes.*"

He tensed and came with a low groan, filling her in long, rough strokes.

Floating on the heady high, Vesper pulled him down beside her and kissed him, pressing her forehead against his sweat-dampened chest. She let out a pent-up breath and felt her eyes drift closed.

Kirael wrapped an arm around her, cradling her against his chest as he moved to lay on his side. Pulling the blankets up around them, he kissed her forehead.

Silence reigned, but it was comfortable. Vesper let it lull her, soothe her, and soon she drifted off...

Wondering what Kirael was thinking.

Wondering if she'd betrayed Mercy, taking this hour's pleasure while her sister was held captive in Hell.

Wondering whether she'd regret tonight in the bright light of the morning.

More likely, whether Kirael would regret it...

19

KIRAEL

Waking with Vesper in his arms was an experience Kirael would never forget. Her soft, warm body cradled in his arms, her soft vanilla scent invading his senses. It moved him, though he didn't have the words to describe the way he felt, holding her like this.

She stirred slightly when he did, and his body immediately reacted. He was hard in an instant, and embarrassed of how easily Vesper managed to rob him of his hard-fought self-control. Even in sleep, she called to him on the deepest of levels, making him *want*.

Not just her body, either, though it was more incredible with every glance he got.

No, there was something about Vesper, something he couldn't define. The singular quality that drew him in, the comfort he felt with her, enough to let himself get this close.

Too close, he thought, closing his eyes for a moment. *This is wrong, and I know it. How can I possibly hope for redemption if I can't even do right by the woman I...*

He paused. *Care for*, he finished, careful even in his own thoughts.

Kirael gave himself another minute. One final minute to hold Vesper, to imagine, to get all the *what if*s out of his system.

And then, careful not to disturb her, he disentangled himself. Rising from the bed, he grabbed some clothes and went out in the hallway to dress. He didn't slow down or look back, the lure of what he left behind was too strong.

Patrol, he thought. *And plan for tonight. Pray for the miracle you're going to need to get Vesper and her sister out of Hell alive. That's all you can do right now.*

Lacing up his boots, he pushed himself out into the early morning light, feeling raw and...

Lonely. For the first time since his early days in Hell, he felt completely and utterly alone.

He pushed himself hard the whole day, taking it upon himself to clean out a nest of Vampyres who'd been luring innocent humans into their grasp, leaving their drained and lifeless bodies on the streets.

Then he tracked a Drisegel demon from the French Quarter into the Gray Market, finding its nest and three zombified missing children sleeping in its lair, waiting for Heaven only knew what kind of grim fate.

As the sun began to set, he went to Mere Marie's to check in with Ezra and Lucan. Pulling out his phone, he was surprised to find a text from Vesper.

See you at Madam White's, was all it said.

He blew out a breath, pacing the foyer in Mere Marie's mansion.

"Can I give you some advice?" Mere Marie asked, appearing from seemingly nowhere.

Kirael gave her a look. "If you must."

"You're struggling because of the girl, right?"

He hesitated, then shrugged. "Somewhat. I am trying not to drag her into all of this."

"You're not an angel anymore," she said. "You do know that, right?"

"Of course I do," he said, frowning.

"Are you sure? Because I think you're following some of the Old Testament rules, and you don't have to. Angels may not have soul mates, but nearly every Kith creature does. Including whatever the heck Vesper is."

"What do you mean?" he asked, taken aback. "She's human."

"She's more than that, for sure. Don't know what, though. Not demon, not Vampyre. Maybe got some shifter blood or something. I've seen her move, there's no way she's just human."

Kirael crossed his arms. "That's not really the point."

Mere Marie put her hands on her hips. "No, it isn't. My point is that you are moping over a girl, presumably because you think you can't live a normal life. My point is that you aren't a damned angel anymore, and there's more to it than regrets and penitence. There's freedom, too, if you'd just open yourself to it."

Kirael stared her down for several long seconds, mulling over her words.

"Don't ruin your chance to be happy, if that's what Vesper might be for you. That's all I'm saying," Mere Marie told him, wagging a finger. "Now if you're ready, we have some serious ass-kicking to do."

"Right," Kirael sighed. "I'm going to meet you all at Madam White's in an hour, right?"

"Correct," Mere Marie said. "Wait..."

She reached in the pocket of her robe and produced a handful of sweet-smelling sachets.

"Gris-gris?" Kirael asked.

She shrugged. "Call it for good luck, huh? Might come in handy."

"Well... thanks," Kirael said, accepting the packets and shoving them into the pocket of his jeans.

He parted ways with the others, heading to the Gray

Market solo, his thoughts chaotic. What Mere Marie said, the part about freedom, kept ringing in his head.

He thought about Vesper, about how he'd tried to keep himself apart from her... all in the name of *being fair* to her.

But what did Vesper want? What did she deserve?

Heaven, Hell... he'd been caught up in his personal melodrama for so many millennia. It hadn't much occurred to him to look beyond his own needs, beyond his own struggles. In truth, he hadn't even made much of an attempt to discover Vesper's life story, to find out what she fought against day to day.

He was drawn to her, to her strength and resilience, but... he wanted more. It was a complete surprise to him, but he wanted to peel back all of Vesper's layers, understand her, be someone she could lean on.

And that desire was the very opposite of what he'd worked toward for so long. The distant mirage of forgiveness, the idea that if he did enough good deeds, he'd earn his way back into Heaven...

He wanted the impossible.

But was he ready to give it all up, try for something new and meaningful here on Earth? Live in the present, rather than the past?

He simply wasn't sure.

By the time he managed to pull himself out of his thoughts, he was halfway through the Gray Market, only a few blocks from Madam White's. The place was distasteful to him, a Kith brothel where anything and everything could be bought for the right price.

Decadent, sinful. Certainly not a place where Kirael would normally be caught dead, but... of course, this would be the place Stella chose. Stella reveled in being as bad as she could be, in dragging tempted souls down into the dirt, corrupting them so completely that there could be no going back.

He parked and set off on foot. Kirael pulled up short when

he turned the corner in front of Madam White's. Stella and Vesper stood on the wraparound front porch. Each stood with her hands on her hips, giving the other a skeptical look. Stella in her spike heels and outlandishly scandalous dress, a two-piece number in fire engine red, showcasing all kinds of skin. An oversized white leather purse hung on her shoulder, no doubt an expensive designer brand.

Vesper wore black jeans and a sheer white t-shirt, with her hair bound up in a complex-looking braid. She was incredibly beautiful, despite her black boots and her disdainful sneer. Her simplicity was part of what made her so unique and sexy.

"Ladies..." he said as he climbed the stairs.

They both turned to him, looking as though he was the reason they'd been forced to interact. He almost cringed under the force of their glares. Then Stella's face lit up, and Kirael turned to see Lucan bounding up the stairs.

"There you are," Stella said, all of her attention on Lucan. "I don't like when you make me wait, Lucan."

Lucan shot her a frown, but Kirael didn't miss the fact that Lucan's eyes traveled up and down Stella's body more than once. Kirael knew that Stella and Lucan were once an item, passionately in love in fact, but at some point they'd fallen out. These days, Lucan seemed unable to tolerate the sight of her.

"Did you bring everything?" Kirael asked Vesper.

She pointed at her messenger bag, which lay on the porch near her feet. "Got it."

"Let's get going, then," Mere Marie said. "The portal straight to Hell isn't going to open itself."

Stella rolled her eyes. "To be on the safe side, we're going to go through a series bolt-holes first. I've linked them to this..."

She dug a white velvet pouch from her purse, carefully opening it and showing them a delicate glass orb.

"We just touch that, and it will take us... where?" Vesper asked.

Stella huffed. "To the portal I set up for you, obviously.

Lucan and I will stay here. The rest of you will go to the portal, do what you need to do. I hope you've arranged for something to pierce the threshold of the portal."

"Taken care of," Vesper said.

"Whatever. There's another orb on the other end for when you're ready to leave. Hands in, everyone!" Stella said, holding the ball out to them.

Kirael glanced at Vesper, who looked nervous. He held out his hand, ignoring Stella's derisive snort, and Vesper laced her fingers with his.

"On three? One, two, three..." he counted off. They both touched it at the same time.

Kirael felt the world lurch around him. Everything swirled and twisted, then it went completely dark. A few scenes flashed before his eyes, spots where Stella had linked the bolt-holes: a park with a rusting swing set, a smoky night club, a flash of what might have been dense green jungle foliage. In theory, the linked portals would confuse anyone who tried to follow them, possibly even mask their presence before they penetrated the portal into Hell.

Another dozen scenes flashed, too quick for Kirael to take in, and then he felt a gut-wrenching sensation as he landed on his feet in a dark, dusty, cramped space.

"Jesus," Vesper said, waving away some of the dust they'd stirred up. "Is this a tomb?"

They were indeed surrounded by big slabs of stone, almost certainly ancient graves. Atop the closest was another orb, glowing softly on a bed of white velvet.

"At least she gave us a little light," Kirael said with a shrug.

Ezra and Mere Marie popped into existence a second later, coughing and sputtering.

"Oh, this is just beyond the pale," Mere Marie declared as she looked around. "Wow, can't miss the portal, huh?"

The wall to their left wasn't the same dark, rough stone.

Instead it was a wall of pure dense blackness. Strangely, it was as difficult to stare at as the sun itself.

"That's what we're going into?" Vesper asked. Kirael gave her hand a squeeze, then released her.

"We'll be all right," he said.

Vesper set her messenger bag on the nearest stone slab, producing the cross.

Kirael held out his hand and called the vials from his angelic stash, handing them over to Mere Marie. Then he called his sword, which was a cool, heavy comfort in his hand.

"Ah, one more thing," he said, laying his sword at his feet.

He held out both hands and summoned Vesper's twin blades, the gold gleaming dully in the dim light.

"Ah!" Vesper said, a grin lighting up her whole face when he handed them over. "I've missed these."

"Hopefully you'll use them more wisely this time," he said, lips twitching.

"Depends," Vesper said, looking gleeful. "Don't get on my nerves, maybe I won't stab you."

"Alright, everyone," Mere Marie said. "Let's focus."

Ezra hopped up onto the slab, looking a little bored. Mere Marie ushered Kirael and Vesper over to the portal.

"I'm going to throw both vials, one for each of you," the Voodoo Queen told them. "Vesper, you pierce the Veil with the cross, and then y'all better boogie."

"Okay," they said in unison.

Mere Marie held up her hands, murmuring an incantation. The portal began to shift, little veins of silver cracking through it. When Mere Marie uncorked the vial and tossed the contents onto the portal, it went solid as a silver platter, reflective as a mirror.

"Now!" she said, and Vesper shoved the cross against it.

The ornamental cross sailed right through the portal, sucking at Vesper's hand.

"Shit!" she cried.

She stumbled forward, flinging out to grab Kirael. Kirael caught her arm just in time to feel the puuuuuuuuullllllll...

Everything stretched, and Kirael felt himself yanked through the Veil. He and Vesper tumbled onto the ground, winding up in a spot that looked for all the world like a bustling block of downtown New York.

"I... what?" Vesper said, looking around wildly. "Did the spell go wrong?"

"No," Kirael said, standing and helping her up. "We're in Hell, all right."

"But this is... like, normal?" Vesper said, staring at a hot dog vendor standing near them.

"Yeah. This place is Belial's doing," Kirael said. "It's for people who spent their whole lives ranting about how they're expecting a heavenly reward. Bad people who use the cover of religion as a way to condescend and hurt others."

Vesper's eyes widened. "Wow."

"Yeah. There are endless levels, but this one is particularly insidious. Imagine you die, you expect to rise and see the Heavenly Host greeting you. Then you land here... it's just three blocks long, then it starts over. Over and over and over," he said, shaking his head. "Some souls, it just completely destroys them. It's unbearable to watch."

Vesper bit her lip, looking down. "I can't believe we're in Hell. Sometimes my life goes by so fast, and then I stop and think, what did I do to end up here? This is a particularly strong example."

"It's going to be okay," Kirael said, taking her hand again. "Come on, we should keep moving at all times. Harder to hit a moving target."

"How do we get out?" she asked.

"Easy enough, if you're not assigned to be here," he said. "Pick a doorway, any doorway..."

He led her to the nearest door, a busted-looking electronics shop. When they stepped through it, they found themselves in a dark stone tunnel.

"This seems more familiar," Vesper said. "You know where we're going, I assume?"

"Yep. Downward, if you'd believe it," he said. "This is the uppermost part of Hell. We're aiming for the middle, more or less."

"That's where Mercy is?" she asked. "And the thing you need to get?"

"That's the place," he said. He'd barely thought of the Book of Names in the last few days, focusing mostly on Vesper and her needs. Foolish, considering his hopes of returning to Heaven's good graces.

They continued through the tunnels, Kirael leading the way, navigating mostly by picking tunnels that led downward. He was careful to avoid entering any other levels except where they had no choice.

In the end, they went through a world that was nothing but an endless dark stretch with knee-deep water, a level that held a giant house of endless staircases going in all directions like a nightmarish MC Escher painting, and a level that was a wall of nothing but a single big mirror — and the reflections in it were ghastly, highlighting a soul's deepest insecurities and flaws.

His own reflection he knew all too well — he'd come here often in his time serving Lucifer. It was a glimpse of the past, of the moment he chose to defect from Heaven. On loop, over and over and over.

He didn't know what Vesper would see in the mirror, but he'd rather save her that pain.

"Don't look," Kirael said, putting his hand next to Vesper's face. Giving her blinders, essentially. "Please, trust me."

"I trust you," she said softly, letting him guide her through the level.

Though quiet, her words reverberated within him. *I trust you. I trust you.*

His heart gave a funny squeeze, but he pushed the feeling aside. There was absolutely no time for that, not now.

After they made it through and into the tunnels once more, Kirael had to stop to get his bearings. They were very, very close to the Atrium, which held all the private rooms for the Fallen.

On one end, the Book of Names lay in a chamber next to Lucifer's quarters.

Far on the other end of the Atrium lay the houses of ill repute, places where the lower demons and Fallen could gamble, drink, and whore away their endless lives.

Vesper grabbed Kirael's arm, pulling him to a stop in the tunnel. She held up a finger and then pointed to her ear, motioning for him to wait, listen.

At the sound of booted feet, Kirael threw up a shield of privacy. It hid them both from plain sight, but only if someone wasn't really looking for them. It was also limited by only working on lower Fallen and demons, not on the more powerful enemies.

Kirael flattened himself against the rocky wall, motioning for Vesper to do the same. Two figures appeared in the juncture of a nearby tunnel, less than fifty yards from where Kirael and Vesper stood. A Fallen and a demon of some sort.

They slowed, one of the Fallen pausing right where the two tunnels met. Kirael recognized him as Jeremet, a mid-level Fallen who specialized in the very same kind of *wet work* as Kirael used to do.

If Jeremet saw them, he would know Kirael in an instant. Kirael and Vesper would likely be dead where they stood.

"Is there a problem?" the scaly red-skinned Ykinnis demon standing beside Jeremet asked, sounding impatient.

"No, just..." Jeremet frowned, then shook his head. "Nothing."

"As I was saying, if we work together to overthrow Belial..." the demon explained.

The two moved on, their voices fading, and Kirael let out a huge breath.

"That was close," Vesper whispered.

"Too close," Kirael agreed. "I'm glad you heard them. Let's keep moving, but definitely be on the lookout. We're going to see more and more Fallen as we approach the Atrium, which is where your sister will be."

"I—" Vesper started, then stopped. "They're coming back."

Kirael took her hand and led her the opposite way, up the gently sloped tunnel. He could hear several sets of heavy boots again.

"This way," Jeremet ordered. "I swear I sensed an outsider."

Kirael took the next right, in a tunnel that dropped steeply until it fed out into a small rock cupola. The only way forward was to enter another level, and a single glance told Kirael exactly which one it was.

The fine hairs on the back of his neck raised.

Jeremet and the other Fallen were gaining on them. Kirael wanted nothing less than to step into this particular level, but it couldn't be helped.

"Vesper..." he whispered, glancing at her. "Don't let go, okay?"

She looked up at him, her eyes wide and bright with worry. She nodded, and his heart lurched again.

Squeezing her hand, Kirael took a deep breath, then plunged forward through the threshold.

20

VESPER

The space Vesper stepped into was... shocking.

The ground under her feet was still dark stone. All around her, the sky was blank and white, unnatural as could be. She stood on a small clearing of sorts; a hundred yards away, the ground rose to form a thin, high stone arch.

A bridge, if you were the bravest person in the world. Up and up and up it went, Vesper's eyes widening as she took it in. The arch thinned even more at the top, until it was mere inches wide.

Below it, more endless white mist.

"Are we safe?" Vesper asked, glancing behind her.

"They're not coming after us," Kirael said, his voice flat. "No one comes in here willingly. So... safe from Jeremet, perhaps."

"Where are we?"

"The first level Lucifer ever created. Fear."

"Fear?" she asked, incredulous. "That's what you called it? I'm not even afraid of heights."

"This is only the first small piece of the whole level. A test, you could call it." Kirael gave her a long look. "This is going to become very unpleasant."

"Don't you know all the tricks? Can't you get us out a side door or something?" she asked, frowning.

"This isn't an amusement park ride, Vesper. This is Hell. There's no escaping." He closed his eyes for a moment, then sighed. "Whatever happens, you must act decisively. The level is supposed to frighten newcomers, who don't have bodies. Normally, they just learn that their concept of corporality and end the level by accepting that they no longer have a physical form, and that they cannot overcome their fears."

"But we both have... a physical form..." Vesper said, confused.

"Yes. It's going to be more difficult for us. We'll have to overcome our fear in each scenario, I should think."

Vesper glanced at him. "Seriously?"

"This isn't the time for sarcasm, Vesper. Just... don't let your fear rule you. Nothing you see will be real. Since it's not real, you can call up objects to help you, within reason."

"Like... think it, and I'll have it?"

"Something like that. Just be careful. The object here isn't to repress your fear... seeming unafraid will just make things worse. This level is very... intuitive."

"Okay."

"I'll be with you. Let's get moving."

Kirael walked up the stone arch, crossing the narrowest section in a few big steps. He turned to look back at her, raising a brow.

"Why can't we just fly over it?" she asked.

"The challenges grow greater as we progress. If we progress too quickly or easily, mainly through the physical challenges, the later ones will be... very difficult. It's better to go through these than end up with five or six psychological challenges. Believe me."

"Okay. You can do this," she told herself.

She followed Kirael's steps, though the path was so steep in some places that she had to lean in and balance with her hands. She tried her best not to look down, but when the stone path dropped away under her feet and grew narrower than her foot, her heart started to thrum.

The world beneath her was just so *empty*...

She wobbled, feeling the stone shift under her feet.

"Vesper, *focus*," Kirael said.

She took a deep breath, feeling for all the world like a tightrope walker, and pushed herself across the thinnest part. Kirael stood at the other end, holding out his hand. She took a couple of big steps, just as she'd seen him do, and then she was across.

When her fingers touched his, her relief was immense... and very brief.

Suddenly the down slope of the stone arch shifted, leaving Kirael and Vesper each standing on a tiny stepping stone, a sea of steaming red lava all around them. Another small platform stood a few hundred feet away, beckoning.

"Shit," she muttered. "You weren't kidding."

"Come on, we have to keep moving," Kirael said.

"No problem," Vesper said, spotting a free stone and hopping to it, then another. "I was a master of this game as a kid."

"Game?" Kirael asked, following her from stone to stone.

"Yeah. The floor is lava," she said. Heat rose from the lava, sweltering and steaming, and Vesper started to sweat a little.

"I will never fully understand humans," Kirael sighed.

"Almost... there..." she said, taking the last three hops in quick succession. "Done!"

"Mmmhm," Kirael said, landing next to her. "Ah, I think the next one is for me."

Vesper turned around to see... herself. A perfect copy of herself, standing at the top of a very high cliff. Behind her stood an unbelievably handsome blond man, a little smile playing over his lips.

The man held a dagger, pointed straight at the nape of fake

Vesper's neck as she inched toward the cliff's edge, tears running down her face.

"No, please..." fake Vesper mumbled. She turned to look at Vesper and Kirael, pleading. "Won't you save me?"

"Don't," Kirael said, holding out an arm to stop her. "This isn't for your benefit."

"What, this is your fear?" Vesper asked, taken aback.

Kirael shot her a look, then nodded. "Yes."

"So... how do you defeat it?" she asked.

"Just do it, Lucifer!" he shouted. "Put me out of my misery!"

Vesper made a strangled sound, crossing her arms. Kirael arched a brow at her, and she glanced away.

A high scream rent the air as Lucifer shoved fake Vesper off the ledge. Kirael flinched, then blew out a breath. Lucifer disappeared in a puff of smoke, and then the entire world went dark.

Completely, utterly, shockingly dark. Vesper's heart starting thumping again, and she could feel herself blush.

This challenge was for her. Even though she was a grown woman, Vesper was still a teeny bit afraid of the dark. Okay, more than a little bit. It was silly, and she knew it was silly, but that didn't make it less scary.

"Kirael?" she called out, but the darkness seemed to suck her voice from the air.

She shivered, feeling alone in a way she'd never felt before. Everything was still and silent, but that didn't mean that something bad didn't lurk just beyond where she stood.

She thought about what he'd said about summoning objects. Holding out her hand, she imagined herself holding a tall white candle.

Instantly she felt it, her fingers wrapped around a tall column candle. She focused on the point of light it gave off, swinging it toward where she thought Kirael might be standing. But the light was too dim.

She turned in the opposite direction, then gasped. She'd

seen something, a glint of metal. Holding out her candle with a shaking hand, she moved closer, closer...

The light of her candle flickered, then flared high. Vesper gasped; in the low light, she'd caught the briefest glance at a huge monster, all sharp metal scales and darkly dripping teeth.

She whirled, then screamed. Another monster, this one a big lump of pale flesh, a trail of slime oozing from each of its big red eyes.

"Oh god, they're all around me..." she whispered.

She turned again, finding the Vampyre Jacinth standing there, a smudge of blood on his mouth.

Panicking, Vesper stepped back. Instantly, she felt something brush against her jacket, something bump her ankle. The monsters were closing in, ready to attack, take her apart.

She closed her eyes for a second, trying to think. Adrenaline washed through her, making it hard to do anything but run, as far as she could get...

It isn't real, she thought. *None of this is any more real now than it was when you were a kid. You can get rid of them all, if you want to...*

But how? How did you destroy all the monsters at once, lost and alone in complete darkness?

She thought back to when she was a kid. She'd shared a room with her big sister. Bunk beds, in fact. Mercy was never out of reach

Back then, Mercy had always chased the monsters away. Being a year older and therefore wayyyy more mature, Mercy's solution was always simple: turn on the lights.

Vesper could picture it now. Mercy crawling out of bed with an exasperated sigh, picking her way across the toy-strewn floor in the dark, flipping on the lights.

"See, Ves? No more monsters. They're allergic to the light," Mercy always told her.

And it worked, without fail. Vesper always slept deeply after that, knowing Mercy had chased the monsters away.

Standing in the dark, Vesper looked down at her candle.

What if... she thought, an idea coming to her. It was crazy, but...

She crouched, feeling another soft brush against her thigh. Then she very, very carefully stuck the candle out, this way and that...

It caught suddenly, the flame flaring bright. It was Jacinth, the flames bursting over his fancy suit, tearing up to engulf him in flame. He screamed, a high and piercing sound, then shattered, little pieces of flame flying out.

Those pieces caught the monsters next to him, and the fire began to spread. Vesper stood, shielding her eyes, as a hundred different monsters shuffled and groaned, encircling her as they began to burn.

They screamed, then shattered, one by one by one...

Suddenly the whole world melted away, and Vesper stood on that simple rocky clearing once more, Kirael at her side.

"Are you okay?" he asked, rubbing her arm. "You were quiet for a long time."

"Fine, I think..." Vesper said, shaking her head. "That was... intense."

"Mine too," Kirael said with a wince. "I had two challenges. In the first, Metatron hunted me. I had to stand still and let him behead me. In the second... well, let's just say Lucifer is crueler than you could possibly imagine."

"Wait, you had two challenges in the time it took me to have one?" she asked.

Kirael shrugged. "Practice. This isn't my first time in here, not even close."

"I guess that means I'm next..." she said, glancing around. "Oh..."

To her right, a shadowy shape filtered down from the sky, slowly coming together to form a door.

"I can see it," Kirael said. "Which means I might be able to come with you, if you want..."

Grabbing his hand, Vesper towed him to the door. "Let's get this over with. I want to get out of here, *bad*."

"Okay," Kirael said. "Go ahead."

Releasing his hand, she reached out and pushed the door open. It looked like wood, but the door felt cool and smooth under her fingers, like metal. The sensation of it made her think instantly of her least favorite place.

"Shit, we're in the hospital," she said, stepping into a perfectly-replicated patient room.

A frail body lay tucked in the bed. Half a dozen doctors stood on one side of the bed, half a dozen family members on the other.

Unmistakably, Vesper recognized herself as the person closest to the bed. Oddly, she was wearing a skirt and a cardigan, the kind of outfit she'd preferred back in her librarian days. She was holding the patient's hand, tears streaming down her face.

She didn't even have to glance down at the bed to know it was Mercy lying there, or to know that Mercy was dying.

This was the moment she'd expected, the moment she'd dreaded, since the first night Mercy didn't come home. Since the moment she realized what kind of terrible trouble Mercy was in, how dangerous the Kith world could be.

Vesper's heart pounded in her chest. She wanted to close her eyes, or turn around and go back. But when she turned, there was only Kirael, watching her with something like compassion on his face. The door was gone.

There was no leaving now.

"I don't want you to see this," she told Kirael, her voice wobbling.

"It's not real," he said, stepping forward and putting an arm around her shoulders.

"That's the thing..." Vesper said. "It is real. It just hasn't happened yet, you know?"

"Vesper—" he started, but she cut him off.

"No," she said, shaking her head. "You don't understand. Mercy has been like... a *heartbeat* away from this for years. Every single time I get a phone call that I don't recognize, I think... this is it. It's the morgue, calling me to come identify her body."

Vesper felt a tear slip down her cheek. She reached up and brushed it away; she hadn't even realized she was crying until now.

"I'm sorry," Kirael said, pulling her close for a hug.

Vesper closed her eyes and hugged him back, letting him comfort her for a full minute. It felt strange. On one hand, she didn't want anyone to see this part of her life, to know how sad and distant her relationship with Mercy had become.

On the other hand, Kirael wasn't judging her. He wasn't pitying her. He was just... being there. Vesper hadn't ever had someone like that in her life, not since Mercy vanished into the sunset.

It felt... incredible.

She blew out a breath, then opened her eyes. Unless she wanted to stay here forever, she needed to face this head-on, confront and control her fear.

"Okay," she said. "I'm going to need a minute."

"I'll be right here," he said, and she knew his words were true.

She gave him a soft smile, and he leaned down to press a kiss to her lips. Her heart fluttered at the gentle, tender touch. Something stirred in her chest, a kind of knowing, but now wasn't the time for it.

She released Kirael and went to Mercy's bedside. The people there, including her other self, stepped back and gave her space. She took Mercy's hand, just as she'd seen herself do a few moments earlier.

She looked down at her sister, her heart wrenching. Mercy was nothing but skin and bones, the circles under her eyes dark as bruises. Her dark hair was thin and tangled, her lips dry and cracked.

The rise and fall of her slender body as she breathed was so slight, it brought a fresh batch of tears to Vesper's eyes. There was a mask over her mouth, connected to a breathing tube, and several IVs in both of Mercy's arms.

"Ma'am?"

Vesper looked up to find a young doctor standing across from her, handsome in his white coat and blue scrubs.

"Yes?" she asked.

"The machines are breathing for her, keeping your sister alive," he said. "There is nothing more we can do. She's not going to wake up."

"No!" Vesper said, clutching at Mercy's hand.

Suddenly Kirael was at her side. Not touching her, not speaking, just... there. She glanced at him, feeling her face burn.

"I don't want her to die," she admitted to Kirael.

"I know," he said.

"I just... I don't know how to end this," she said.

"Say what you need to say to Mercy. Then... I think you have to let her go," he said, looking pained.

"Right. Right." She took a breath, then looked down at Mercy again. "Mercy..."

She stopped, took another big breath, released it. This was harder than she could've imagined.

"Mercy, I'm so sorry," she blurted out, wiping away tears. "I'm so sorry that this happened to you. I know we didn't have a great life, growing up. I know you took a lot of the burden, protecting me, taking care of me. I just... I know you're hurting. That's why I..."

She paused, took another breath.

"That's why I never tried that hard to stop you, when I first found out you were sneaking down to the Gray Market to score drugs. I just figured... you'd had it rough, maybe you deserved to let loose."

She let her head drop, sorrowful.

"I am so, so sorry for that, Mercy. I wish I'd tried to stop you back then, before you got hooked. I wish I'd been able to keep you off the street. I wish I could have been strong enough to stop all of the bad things that happened to you. When we were kids, after you got in with the Vampyres... It's killed me, watching this happen to you."

She carefully laid Mercy's hand back on the bed, then reached out to brush back a lock of her sister's hair.

"I've been so angry with you," Vesper admitted, her tears flowing freely. "I've hated you, as much as I love you. I feel so guilty all the time, and I can't do anything about it."

She straightened, wiping her face with her sleeve, then sighed.

"Maybe this is what you wanted, to be free of it all?" Vesper told Mercy. "I hope you are at peace, big sister. I love you, a lot. More than you knew, I think."

Silence lapsed. There were a million more things she wanted to say. Stories she wanted to recount, regrets she felt she should name.

And yet, she didn't say any of them. She just stood there, staring at Mercy for several minutes.

Finally, she looked up at Kirael, then at the doctor.

"I think..." she started, feeling that strange kind of empty she only ever felt after a lot of crying. "I think I'm ready."

The doctor nodded, turning and pressing several buttons, turning off some alarms as they started to blare. Everyone stood and watched as Mercy's chest rose and fell, rose and fell...

And didn't rise again.

Vesper heard a distressed sound coming from her own throat. She reached out for Kirael and he was there, taking her hand, grounding her.

A monitor started beeping, showing that Mercy's heart had stopped beating.

"God damn it, Mercy," Vesper whispered, shaking her head.

Then, like a dream, the whole scene faded before her eyes. Vesper blinked, looking around. They were in the same small clearing, except now there was a glowing white portal beckoning to them.

"Is that it?" she asked.

"I think so," Kirael said, nodding. "I suppose we made it through."

Hand in hand, they walked to the portal, stepping through it. They ended up in another stone tunnel, and Vesper let out a breath.

"Thank god," she sighed. "I've never been so glad to leave anywhere, I think."

"Don't get too comfortable," Kirael said. "We're almost to the Atrium, but we haven't yet begun to fight."

On impulse, Vesper gave him a quick, tight hug.

Kirael arched a brow. "What was that for?"

"Just... I'm glad you're here with me, that's all."

He looked for a moment as though he wanted to say something, but then he just shook his head. "Me too, Vesper."

Then he turned and led her onward, deeper into the viper's nest.

21

KIRAEL

Kirael pulled up short when he saw the softly glowing night sky at the end of the tunnel. The Atrium was only a stone's throw away now

"Okay, remember the plan," Kirael told Vesper. "I am going to take you to the brothel. You're going to extract your sister without drawing too much attention to yourself. I'm going to go do what I need to do and try not to get killed."

"Then you're coming back for us, unless you get caught," Vesper said, worry creasing her face.

"Yes. If I get caught, it would actually be better for you two. It would provide a huge distraction, no one would even notice you escaping."

"Assuming we could figure out how... this place is a giant stone labyrinth, and I absolutely cannot drag Mercy through any of the levels we went through." Vesper's brow knitted. "I hadn't considered it, but what if she can't even walk?"

"Let's cross that bridge if and when we come to it, okay?" Kirael said.

"Right. Yes. Think positive," Vesper said, but he could already hear the defeat in her voice.

The last level had really shaken her, and Kirael wished like anything he knew what to do or say to bring back her confidence. He needed her at her best if they were going to pull this thing off.

"Okay," he said, holding out his hands. He summoned two garments into his hands: a full cloak for himself, and an oversized head scarf for her.

Head scarves were worn by the few unfortunate humans who served in Hell. Blood slaves like Vesper's sister, or kidnapped lovers of powerful Fallen. The scarves were different colors, depending on the human's worth.

He'd chosen navy for Vesper, meaning she was not important enough to draw attention, but that she belonged to someone who would be upset if she were hurt or killed.

It also covered the twin short swords strapped to her shoulders, a convenient second use.

For himself, he chose a simple dark cloak, something that a mid-level demon might wear. Lucifer despised ugliness in any form, and would not have it present outside the levels. Any demon without beautiful humanoid features often wore a cloak in the Atrium to avoid Lucifer's sudden and violent tempers.

Kirael and Vesper both put on their respective garments, making sure their weapons were close at hand.

"Ready?" he asked.

"Ready," Vesper said.

"You have your watch?" he asked.

She pulled back her sleeve, showing off the chunky plastic wristwatch she'd worn for the mission. Kirael pulled back his own sleeve, showing his watch, and they took a moment to sync the times.

Then he ushered her down the tunnel and out into the Atrium. He heard Vesper stifle a gasp, and understood perfectly why.

The Atrium was stunningly beautiful, a blanket of dazzling

sky above and little clusters of buildings below, all done in different styles.

"Are we supposed to be in Rome?" Vesper whispered.

"Lucifer grew jealous of humanity's ability to create things of such beauty. He took a little piece of each great city and replicated them all down here, in one place. Rome, Paris, Constantinople, Cairo, Jericho, Beijing."

"Wow. Which part is Mercy in?"

"Constantinople."

"And your errand?"

"None of them. The Fallen live in a replica of the same palace we inhabited in Heaven."

Vesper glanced at him, surprised.

"Keep your head down," he warned her. "It's best if we don't talk."

They walked for several minutes in silence before they reached the brothel. The scenery changed, shifting from the column-filled piazzas of Rome to the soaring red-roofed majesty of Constantinople.

Kirael raised his hand to point at a building as they passed it. A neat chalk X was drawn above the door, as their informant had promised.

"Okay," Kirael said, drawing Vesper over to the side. "In and out, as little contact as possible. Keep your head down, don't speak unless spoken to, unless you absolutely must. Then you go to the safe house."

"Got it."

"Vesper," he said, gripping her shoulders. "If I'm not back in an hour, you and Mercy have to find your own way out."

She looked up at him, her emerald gaze darkening. "I don't want to leave you."

"You won't have a choice. I promise, if I don't return, I will be dead. They'll have to kill me to keep me from coming back to you, do you understand?"

Her lips trembled, but she nodded. "Yes."

Glancing around, he decided to take a risk. Leaning close, he kissed her lips, quick and firm.

"Go," he said. "Be careful."

I don't know what I will do if something happens to you, was his thought, but he didn't dare voice it aloud.

"You too," she said.

Pulling her head scarf down to cover more of her face, Vesper turned and vanished around the corner, heading for the servants' entrance.

Kirael forced himself to walk away, to keep his pace normal as he left Constantinople. He moved to the very edge of the cityscape, skirting the whole area in an attempt to avoid any Fallen or high level demons. He even hunched down a little, trying to make himself smaller and less noticeable.

Soon he was past the city and closing in on the palace. He'd explained it to Vesper as being an exact replica as the palace of the Heavenly Host, but he'd left out one detail: it was all done in black.

Black marble, black metal, black stone, sitting on an eerie black cloud. The product of Lucifer's too-literal early interpretation of what it meant to rebel against Heaven, in Kirael's opinion.

Looking back on the Fall, much of Lucifer's behavior reminded Kirael of an angst-filled teenager, seeking to test boundaries and anger authority figures. At the time, he'd thought Lucifer was going to create a new world, a world that was just and righteous.

Instead, Lucifer had shown himself to be rotten down to the very core, corrupting everything he touched. Ruling Hell with a malevolent, violent cronyism that made even the earliest humans look like a wise, peace-loving tribe.

Kirael walked right into the palace. Between his cloak and the shambling walk he adopted as he made his way up the grand black marble staircase, no one even spared him a glance.

Inside, it was as though the palace of Versailles had been

redecorated by a Goth with baroque leanings. All heavy, dark furniture, endless hallways running up and down the length of the place. There were communal dining and lounge areas in the middle of the palace, but Kirael wasn't going near those.

As he headed all the way to the right side of the building, various demons and Fallen rushed to and fro, carrying out their daily tasks. Lucifer's quarters were located at the very back of the palace, built into the bedrock of Hell.

Lucifer's chamber was the most fortified place in all of the Atrium. Numerous guards and locked vault doors guarded the room. Plus, if the alarm was raised, the whole palace was packed to the gills with Fallen ready for battle.

Kirael kept his head down and pushed forward. He needed the Book, the reason he started this whole mad crusade in the first place. He didn't slow until he turned down the hallway where Lucifer's rooms lay.

The guards were midlevel Fallen, standing calmly outside the door to Lucifer's antechamber. Kirael walked right past them, then summoned his sword.

Whirling, he took them both down in a matter of seconds, practically in near silence. He took care not to kill either of them, instead knocking them out.

Vanishing his sword, he pulled out the set of keys that the Shkisa demon passed on to him. He unlocked the heavy black wood door, then stepped inside. Dragging the two guards inside, he summoned a length of cord and tied them both hand and foot, ensuring that they wouldn't be a problem.

Kirael stood and looked around. He'd never entered Lucifer's rooms before; only Belial was allowed the privilege. The antechamber was empty except for three huge doors. One gold, one silver, one black.

This, Kirael had not anticipated. The gold, he assumed, was the bedroom. It would be very much like Lucifer to have a lavish, color-saturated private chamber reserved for himself, while everyone else lived in monotones.

He walked over to the black door, raising a hand. Before he could even lay a hand on it, all the hair on his body rose, prickling with alarm. He backed away, surprised.

Whatever was in that room... Kirael wanted nothing to do with it.

Pulling out the keys again, he saw that only one was silver. He made quick work of unlocking the silver door and letting himself inside.

His jaw dropped a little when he saw the room's contents.

The door was obviously a bolt-hole, because inside was a strange scene. A stunning green pasture, sun shining down, horses roaming in the distance.

The only two things in the immediate area were a tree and a glass structure that held a heavy book, pages bared. The Book of Names, Kirael assumed.

The tree caught his interest for a moment, though. It was perfectly lifelike but black as night, with shining red apples hanging low. He walked closer to the tree, the sudden desire to taste that fruit blooming within him.

He raised his hand, even going so far as to cup his fingers around the apple, but something stopped him. His interest was too strong, too sudden. It was pure, carnal temptation.

Not quite understanding what he was feeling, Kirael forced himself to step back. He had to drag each foot to move back another step, the tree's lure was so strong.

Lucifer, he thought. *This tree is... or has... his essence, somehow.*

Turning, he propelled himself toward the Book. He made it to the Book, flipping it closed in a swift movement. His fingers trailed over the engraved title, inscribed in Aramaic, but it was certainly the right tome.

Kirael hefted it, running his fingers over the smooth black leather. He held it out in his hands, attempting to vanish it, but no luck. The book weighed on him, in a strange way. The more he looked at it, the stronger his desire to return to the tree became.

I've got to get out of this room, he realized. *I have to get back to Vesper, protect her.*

The image of Vesper's face, the way she'd looked at him just before he left her at the brothel, helped him focus. The twenty steps to the door were some of the hardest Kirael ever took, but he managed it.

Stepping through the threshold was like emerging from the depths of a frozen lake. He sucked in a deep breath, taking a moment to stop and catch his breath.

Straightening, he held out the book, this time managing to vanish it. One of the guards was awake, wiggling and calling out. Kirael looked at him.

"I know you. Drishael, right? Listen, don't make me knock you out again. I'm already out the door anyway."

Drishael looked at Kirael, then at the other guard. He stayed silent.

"Good man," Kirael said, leaving Drishael behind on the floor. He pulled up the hood of his cloak again and slipped out of the antechamber.

As he left the hallway, turning off into another part of the palace, he passed two more Fallen. No doubt they would soon notice the missing guards, which meant that Kirael needed to get out of the palace, fast.

He trotted down every empty hall he found, wondering how much time he had to meet Vesper. He exited the palace, trying not to feel too excited. After all, he still had to escape Hell with two others in tow.

Glancing up at the clock tower looming in the distance, he cursed aloud. He only had five minutes remaining to meet Vesper at the safe house. Time must have run differently in the bolt-hole, but no matter.

Tucking his head down to keep his hood in place, Kirael began to *run*.

22

VESPER

Clutching at her head scarf, trying to keep her steps at a normal pace, Vesper walked around the back of the blood brothel. Now that she was here, on the verge of finding Mercy, she began to tremble.

Without Kirael at her back, anxiety truly set in. The building itself was a neat three-story stone affair, something that wouldn't have been out of place, perhaps, in the oldest parts of London.

She found the servants' entrance at the back, just as Kirael said. At the right of the door was a simple silver plaque that read: Drisgell House — Ring Bell For Assistance.

Biting her lip, she tried the door. To her immense relief, she found it unlocked. Easing it open, she stepped inside. Pulling a piece of paper from her pocket, she jammed it in the door lock, making sure she'd be able to leave again.

Taking a deep breath, she turned and scanned the dark, silent hallway before her. She'd talked this part through with Kirael. He didn't frequent them himself, but he'd been inside them before.

She couldn't just walk through, opening doors until she

found her sister. She'd do a quick examination, get as far inside as she could, and when she eventually talked to someone... she'd lie her ass off.

The ground floor proved uninteresting, mostly storage and a big kitchen. A couple of women worked in the kitchen, but Vesper swept right past them, heading for the stairs at the far end of the hallway. When she reached them, she realized that there were two sets of stairs. One simple and worn, one gleaming and polished.

One for staff and one for customers, then. She took the staff stairs, thinking it prudent to chance a confrontation with a servant than to run into an important Fallen or demon.

She went straight up to the third floor. Kirael said that most of the slaves were kept in rooms upstairs, so that was her target. She emerged onto the third floor, immediately spotting a woman in a head scarf at the far end of the long, door-lined hall.

When the woman didn't notice her right away, Vesper tried the first door to her right. It opened and she slipped inside, gasping when she saw a hulking male leaning over an unconscious woman.

"Hey!" he cried, turning to glare at her.

A Vampyre. She could handle this.

"The owners sent me up to you," she blurted out. "I'm... fresh."

The Vampyre scowled, wiping blood from his mouth. On the bed, the girl he'd been feeding from stirred and moaned.

"Let me see your face," he said.

Vesper reached up and drew her scarf down, her stomach turning at the way the Vampyre's face lit up. "Fresh, you said...?"

"Yes, let me just..." she pretended to fumble with her scarf, moving toward him.

At the last moment, she pulled her swords, burying them in

his chest. He let out a shocked gurgle, clutching at her arms, but Vesper gave both swords a sharp twist.

She felt nothing as he dropped to the floor, or as she made quick work of removing his head. Nothing but disgust, and perhaps a grim determination.

He went up in a sulfurous billow of smoke, the close quarters making Vesper cough.

She turned to find the girl blinking at her. She was half-naked, her white night dress ripped open at the chest, a thin rivulet of blood running down from her neck.

"Who are you?" the girl rasped.

"No one. Do you know Mercy?" she asked.

Vesper moved over, dragging a thin blanket over the girl's body. The girl didn't even flinch; her enlarged pupils and too-sweet scent said she was high as a kite.

The girl blinked, then slowly nodded.

"What room is she in?" she asked.

"Two down..." the girl said, closing her eyes.

"Thanks. Don't... don't call out, okay?" Vesper said, but the girl was already asleep, or unconscious again maybe.

It took everything in Vesper's soul to make herself leave the girl there like that, but there was nothing for it. Brushing the last bits of Vampyre dust off herself, she sheathed her swords and left the room.

"You can't be here," said a voice.

She turned to find the same servant standing just to her left, staring at her.

"Oh, I—" Vesper started, then faltered.

"You can't be here without a head scarf," the woman said.

Vesper pulled up her scarf immediately, eyeing the servant. She could only see a few inches of the woman's wrinkled face, but the sound of her voice was... vacant.

"Sorry," Vesper said. "I'm just here to retrieve a girl for... Jeremet."

She took a risk, naming the Fallen that had chased her and Kirael earlier.

The servant stared at her, then bowed and turned away.

Vesper tried not to look shocked. She hadn't actually expected that to work. Then again, if this place wanted tighter security, they shouldn't rely on drug-addled slaves.

Moving down the hallway, she opened what she prayed was Mercy's door. There was no client in this room, at least... just a sleeping form under a pile of blankets.

Vesper crept over to the bed, drawing back the blanket. A horrified sound flew from her mouth at the sight of her sister, thin and bruised and shivering.

"Mercy," she whispered, her voice breaking a little. "Hey, Mercy..."

She reached out and shook her sister's shoulder. Mercy rolled over, showing Vesper the full extent of her injuries. She was covered with black bruises, the after-effects of vicious bite marks, all over her arms and neck and chest.

"Ves?" Mercy asked, her eyelids fluttering open. "Am I in Heaven?"

"Oh, honey..." Vesper said, blinking away the tears that stung her eyes. "I'm here to take you home, okay?"

"I can't leave," Mercy said, closing her eyes. "I'm *his* now."

"Okay, don't worry about that," Vesper said. A thousand questions came to mind, but there was no time. "Come on, I'm gonna help you up."

She drew back the sheets, cringing at the mottled black and blue marks all over Mercy's body.

"How'd you get here?" Mercy asked. "You're not supposed to be here."

Likely, Mercy didn't even know where she was.

"I'll tell you later. Come on. Do you have shoes?" Vesper asked.

"Don't need 'em," Mercy sighed. "Besides, it doesn't matter. He's gonna take care of me..."

Vesper helped her sit up and swing her legs over the bed.

"Sure, honey. Can you walk? Here, let me just put my arm around you, okay?"

Vesper got Mercy upright, then looked around. There was little in the room except a second twin bed, so Vesper stripped the dark-colored top sheet off the spare bed and wrapped it around Mercy, making sure to cover her head.

"Where are we going?"

"Just for a walk," Vesper said.

"I don't think you're real," Mercy said. "I always think you're here, but you never are."

"Shhh, it's okay. Come on, quickly now," Vesper said. "Remember that game we played as kids, hide and seek?"

"Course. I always won," Mercy slurred.

"Yeah, well we're gonna do that, but while we take our walk. So we're gonna be really sneaky, okay?" Vesper said.

"Kay."

Sucking in a lungful of air, Vesper opened the door and stuck her head out into the hall. It was empty, so she hurried Mercy out and toward the stairs. Mercy was slow and clumsy, each movement jerky.

"You got this, Mercy," Vesper said. "Come on, now."

Vesper half-carried her all the way downstairs. Mercy was painfully thin, making Vesper's job all too easy. To Vesper's complete shock, she actually got her sister all the way to the back door without incident.

So close... she thought.

Pulling open the back door, she dragged Mercy outside.

"Ves..." Mercy moaned.

"Shhh, just a little further," Vesper said.

"I can't leave him, Ves."

"Who, honey?"

Vesper waited until a cloak-wearing demon shambled passed them, not even looking up, and then pulled Mercy across the street.

"Lucifer," Mercy said.

"It's okay, you don't have to," Vesper said, too preoccupied to work through her sister's words.

"He loves me."

"Okay."

"He really does."

"Sure, honey," Vesper said.

"Said I'm his favorite girl, because of you," Mercy said in a near-singsong.

"What?" Vesper asked, stopping. "You know what, I want you to tell me all about it once we're inside again."

"Kay."

They moved down the street, Mercy slowing things down so much that Vesper started to sweat under her clothes. It took almost ten minutes to make the two blocks from the brothel to the safe house, and getting Mercy up the front steps was a Herculean task in itself.

Finally Vesper flung open the door of the safe house, pushing her sister inside before slamming it behind them. Vesper flattened herself against the door, pressing her hand against her hammering heart.

Mercy slunk to the floor, and Vesper let her.

"Don't move," Vesper cautioned her sister, pushing herself off the wall. "I'll be right back."

Vesper took a minute to check out the house. It was a simple apartment, entirely empty. The windows and door were all papered over, like someone was about to paint the walls. After a moment, Vesper returned to Mercy.

"How are you feeling?" she asked, crouching down next to where Mercy sat, staring vacantly.

"Mmm. Tired. Need a fix," Mercy mumbled. "He promised he'd bring me something really good. We should go to him."

"Later, Mercy."

"He talks about you, you know? I get jealous."

"Who?"

"Lucifer," Mercy said, losing patience. "You never listen when I talk."

"I'm listening. He talks about me?"

"Yeah. He said he knows what we are," Mercy said, absently rubbing a piece of her makeshift sheet cloak between her fingers.

"What you mean?" Vesper asked, reaching out to trace a bruise on Mercy's wrist.

"Ow, don't!" Mercy said, shooting her a glare. "He said I'm not gonna get these bites anymore, cause we're so special. That's why I'm his girl. He said he was gonna bring you here, too. So we could both be his girls."

"Lucifer said that?" Vesper asked, feeling a chill run through her blood.

"Yep. He said we were gonna have the nicest life. Immortals deserve a really nice life, since it's so long, you know?"

Vesper shook her head. "Okay, Mercy."

"Don't be like that. You never believe me."

"I do. I'm just... worried, right now. We have to take a long walk, and I'm not sure how we're going to do that."

Mercy flapped a hand at her, but Vesper was distracted by a quiet sound from just outside. Grabbing Mercy by the shoulders, she hushed her sister as she dragged her away from the door, motioning for her to stay quiet.

Pulling out one of her short swords, Vesper crept to the door, putting her eye right up to the peep hole. Outside, several Fallen were striding down the street, coming in the direction of the brothel.

One of them called to the others, and they all split in different directions, trotting and looking around.

"Shit," Vesper whispered.

They were definitely hunting for someone, though whether it was for Mercy or for Kirael, Vesper couldn't know.

Kirael, where are you? she wondered. She checked her watch, chewing her bottom lip, then put her sword back in its shoulder sheath.

It was three minutes past the time he'd insisted that she run. Vesper started to panic; there was no way she leaving without him. Not only was Mercy simply too loopy to run for it, but she couldn't even consider the alternatives.

She paced the floor, jumping at every little sound, checking the peephole again and again. Her breath caught when one of the Fallen strode through the yard, glancing at the front door. Luckily he didn't slow, just kept moving.

"Vesper."

Vesper nearly jumped out of her skin. She turned to find Kirael walking into the room.

She immediately ran over to him and flung her arms around him, hugging him tight. Her face heated, but the relief she felt at seeing him just couldn't be expressed in words.

He wrapped his arms around her, holding her close for a long moment. Vesper wanted nothing more than to hold him, to close her eyes and then open them again to find herself far, far away from here.

"How did you get in?" she asked, confused. There was only one door, after all.

"Basement window. The Fallen are out in force, I had to be careful."

"Looking for you, or for Mercy?" she asked.

"Both, probably," Kirael said. "You broke your promise, you know."

"What?"

"I'm late. You should have left already," he said, releasing her and stepping back to give her a look.

"I wouldn't do that," she said, a little hurt. "Besides, Mercy's not doing so hot."

They both glanced over to Mercy, who was slumped against the wall, mouth wide open as she slept.

"Alright. The search is going to spread wider soon enough, and then we'll make a break for it," Kirael said, running a hand through his hair. "I won't lie, it's going to be pretty tough."

He peeled back a bit of the paper at one of the windows and glanced out, his expression dubious. She could see the wheels turning.

"I need you to promise me something," she said.

He dropped the paper and looked at her, arching a brow.

"What's that?" he asked.

"No heroics," she said. "None of this, *I'll distract them while you run* stuff."

Kirael's face went stormy. "Vesper..."

"I mean it. I want to get out of here more than anything, but I don't want it without you."

They were both silent, looking at each other, a thousand unsaid things between them.

"I can't promise that," he said, his gaze intent on hers.

"Kirael... I know we're in a very uncertain situation, but... I don't want to go home to a world without you in it."

"You'd rather die down here, then?" he asked, crossing his arms.

"No, I'd rather we all stick together, no matter what. Call me crazy, but I'm still hoping we can pull this off."

"Vesper, I just..." he started.

"No! This is not the time and place for your bullshit about *unclean hands* and *what I deserve*. Please, Kirael." She moved closer, placing a hand on his chest. "I'm not saying marry me, I'm just saying... I want you in my life. You make me feel good, and... that doesn't come around very often. Or ever, actually."

Kirael cupped her jaw, leaning down to give her a quick, fierce kiss. He closed his eyes, leaning his forehead against hers, looking nothing short of tormented.

"This is where you say, *I like you too*, or something," Vesper told him.

His eyes snapped open, twin pools of blue ice.

"I don't like you."

Vesper scowled, trying to pull away from him.

"Stop," he said, catching her hands. "I just... *like* isn't close to the word for how I feel about you. Maybe there isn't a word for it, yet."

She stopped resisting, letting herself lean into him once more.

"Oh yeah?" she asked, her face going red.

"Yes."

"I guess that's all right, then," she said. Tipping up her face, she pulled him close for another kiss, sucking in a breath to inhale his heady, masculine scent.

Damn, I really might love him, she thought, smiling against his lips.

"Later," Kirael said, pulling away. "When we're not in mortal danger and all."

"You still haven't made that promise," Vesper said, shooting him a look.

"I think it's about time to move," Kirael said, glancing out the window again. "A whole troop of Fallen just went toward the palace, which means we're about to draw Lucifer's attention."

"Yikes."

"Yeah." He glanced over at Mercy. "Is she going to be okay?"

Vesper raised a shoulder. "I don't really know. She was babbling, saying crazy stuff."

"Alright. Put your head scarf back on. I'll carry her, try to hide her under my cloak the best I can," he said. "We just have to make it to the tunnels."

"Right," Vesper said. "Right. Okay."

Kirael went over and picked up Mercy, the tenderness in his movements nearly brought tears to Vesper's eyes again. She helped him pull his cloak over most of Mercy's body as he cradled her close.

Kirael gave Vesper a tight smile, and she returned it.

"Let's do this thing," she said.

"Lead the way... and keep your swords close."

Drawing both gleaming, gold swords, Vesper opened the door and strode out into the open.

23

KIRAEL

They only made it about halfway to the tunnels before Kirael saw an unwelcome face: Jeremet, walking down the steps of another brothel. Kirael's invisibility shield wouldn't work on Jeremet, or not for long anyway.

The other Fallen stopped mid-step when he saw them, his whole body going rigid with interest. He was several blocks away, but far too close for Kirael's comfort.

"Shit. Ten o'clock," Kirael said.

Vesper nodded; she'd already clocked Jeremet and was taking a sharp right turn to avoid heading straight for him. She broke into a trot, not bothering to hide her swords.

"Don't let them drive us back into the center of the Atrium," Kirael said, readjusting Mercy in his arms. "That's what they'll try to do."

"Can we fly?" she asked.

"No. I can't fight and carry both of you, the Fallen would tear us apart midair."

"Right," she said. At the end of the block, she went left again.

"We're really close," Kirael promised. "Don't panic."

"I'm not," she said, preoccupied.

Another two blocks, and Kirael could actually see the dark stone tunnels ahead. Behind them, a cry rang out.

They'd been spotted, and a Fallen was calling the others to the chase.

A glowing green Aetrin demon sprung out in Vesper's path, hissing and spitting venom. Vesper didn't flinch or hesitate. She beheaded the thing in three seconds flat, not even slowing as she let the body drop to the ground.

Kirael's heart swelled. No delicate flower, his Vesper.

Perhaps, if they did make it out, there was a real chance for something between them. Maybe Vesper was tough enough to handle him, sins and all.

"Kirael, they're gaining on us," she shouted back over her shoulder. "Can you run?"

"Yes," he said, shifting Mercy to make movement easier. "Go!"

Vesper broke into a sprint, Kirael right on her heels. In his peripheral vision, Kirael sensed Fallen and demons coming from behind them, from the left and right, too.

"Go!" he shouted again.

Swords flying like a golden blur, Vesper ran flat-out, making it into the mouth of the tunnel.

"Don't stop!" Kirael urged. "Turn! Keep moving!"

Their pursuers dropped back for a moment, bottlenecked by the tunnel entrance. Kirael scrambled for a destination, somewhere they could go to hide...

"Left!" he said, an idea forming. "Go left, and up when you can!"

They twisted and turned until the sound of footsteps behind them quieted, then died away.

"Okay, okay, slow down," he said, struggling for breath.

Vesper stumbled to a stop, leaning against a wall, chest heaving. Kirael put Mercy down, then dropped his hands to his knees. They both stayed like that for a full minute, recovering.

"We didn't die," Vesper said, sounding surprised.

"No."

"Can we get back to the portal from here?" she asked.

"Fuck it," Kirael said, shaking his head and standing up again. "We need to go to plan B."

"And what's plan B?" Vesper asked, sheathing her blades and wiping at her forehead.

"I'm not completely sure," Kirael admitted. "But I know where we should go while we try to figure it out."

Once they'd collected themselves, Kirael picked up Mercy again and took the lead. The Void wasn't far; their haphazard escape had brought them within a quarter mile of it. He led them vaguely up, the tunnels growing familiar as he went.

"Ah, here we are…" he said. "Don't freak out, okay?"

Vesper gave him an unamused look. "Just go in."

They stepped through the portal, coming out onto the broad rock shelf and endless sea of white nothingness that Kirael knew so very well.

"Holy shit…" Vesper said.

She walked out toward the edge, seemingly drawn to it in the same way Kirael was.

"It's something, huh?" he said.

There was a small area of wall and floor to one side, and Kirael felt it reasonably safe to put Mercy down. When he knelt to set her down, she opened her eyes.

"Is he here?" she asked. "I *need* something. Just a little bit."

Kirael stood, looking at Vesper.

"She means drugs," Vesper said, her voice gone flat. "We'll deal with that later. The withdrawal will be… bad."

Kirael walked over to join her at the edge, staring out at the seething mist.

"It's lovely, in a strange way," Vesper said.

"I agree."

They were quiet, in a comfortable way. Both coming down from the adrenaline rush, reeling from the insanity of the last day.

Vesper's stomach made a sound, and she snorted.

"I know, I know," she muttered to her body. "I will feed you at some point, I promise."

Kirael's lips lifted, but his thoughts started to circle.

"When she says *he*..."

"Hmm?" Vesper asked.

"Your sister. *Is he coming*, she said."

"She thinks she and Lucifer are in love. And that she's immortal, or something. I don't know," Vesper said with a shrug.

Kirael's brows shot up. "Why would she think that?"

"Because it's true," came a low, silky voice.

Crisp British accent, smarmy tone... it could only be one person.

Vesper and Kirael both turned to see Lucifer himself standing in front of the portal, looking beyond smug. Dark suit, dark shirt, hair slicked back. It was the uniform of Hell, and no one wore it better than Lucifer.

"Lucifer," Kirael said, his hands clenching into tight fists.

Hadn't this always been his fate? His punishment, for the sin of choosing the wrong side during the Fall? The only shock was his immediate and intense fury at Vesper being involved in the whole thing.

"Kirael. Can't say I'm terribly glad to see you," Lucifer said, straightening his shirt cuffs. "You, on the other hand..."

He gazed at Vesper with avid interest, looking her up and down. Kirael saw Vesper's shudder, caught her quick, helpless glance. He wanted to go to her, comfort her, but that would only give Lucifer more incentive.

Desperation clawed through him. He needed to strike a bargain, and quickly. Lucifer couldn't resist a deal, if it would cause pain and suffering.

"Let them leave," Kirael said. "I'll submit to you, willingly."

"Ah!" Lucifer said, laughing politely. "I think not. A rebellious Fallen angel is worthless to me. Whereas these two ladies are... well, priceless."

Lucifer strode forward. Behind him, Belial, Jeremet, and a dozen other Fallen emerged from the Void.

"What are you talking about?" Kirael asked.

His palms started to sweat, he wanted so badly to summon his sword, fight his way out. It was a fool's errand, though. No one could take down this many Fallen alone, and certainly Vesper or Mercy would be harmed in the process.

"Stand your ground," he called to Vesper. He nodded to Belial, who was already trying to circle around and force Vesper away from the edge, out of Kirael's reach.

She didn't react, didn't look at him. Apparently she'd come to the same conclusion, that she didn't want Lucifer to know that she and Kirael had any kind of bond. *Smart girl.*

"Hmmm," Lucifer murmured. "You don't even know what you've got, Kirael. No matter, it's too late for you now."

"What do you want, Lucifer?" Kirael asked.

"What I want? I want us to go back in time, before you betrayed me and defected. Failing that, I want to see you punished. *Mortally.*"

Vesper made a soft noise, but Kirael didn't look away from Lucifer.

"Same deal. You let them go, all the Fallen generals let them go, and I will submit. To death, if that's what you want."

Vesper took half a step forward, then edged right back, glancing at Belial.

"Not a chance," Lucifer said. "Why would I agree to that, when I have everything I want right here?"

He winked at Vesper, who looked like she was about three seconds from spitting at him.

"I have the Book of Names," Kirael said, grasping at straws.

Lucifer stilled, then smiled. "Yes, I heard about your little caper. Like the tree, did you?"

They stared at each other in silence for long moments.

"A deal, then," Kirael said. "For the Book."

Lucifer cocked his head. "I'm listening."

"You agree... not to release them, but that neither woman will be harmed. In any meaning of the word, no tricks."

"In exchange for the Book?" Lucifer asked.

"Yes."

"And you will submit to punishment," he clarified.

"Yes."

"I don't agree to this," Vesper said, looking between them. "Don't I have to agree to this?"

"No," they both said in unison.

Vesper looked genuinely tongue-tied for the first time since Kirael had met her.

Mercy made a small sound. Everyone turned to look at her as she struggled to her feet.

"Lucy, you came!" she said.

Kirael saw a muscle in Lucifer's jaw tic at the nickname. Lucifer opened his arms and beckoned to her. "Come here, darling."

"Mercy, do *not* go to him," Vesper snapped.

Mercy stopped, then made a dismissive sound. "You don't tell me what to do. I'm the big sister, remember?"

"Mercy, please..." Vesper said, but it was too late.

Mercy stumbled over to Lucifer, who wrapped his arms around her, staring at Kirael and Vesper over Mercy's shoulder. His face split with a truly evil grin; he grabbed a fistful of Mercy's hair and shoved her to her knees.

She made a soft sound, accepting it without hesitation.

"There's a good girl," he said once she knelt before him. "You like that, don't you?"

Mercy gave him a long look, then slowly nodded.

"Stay right here, shut your mouth, and I will make sure you get a nice big dose of the good stuff tonight," he said, as if talking to a dog.

Mercy dropped her gaze to the floor, but nodded again.

"So weak," Lucifer sighed.

"You're making a mistake," Vesper said, her words soft but deadly.

"What was that?" Lucifer asked, his gaze snapping to her.

Kirael glared at her, but she shook her head.

"You think this is what you want, but it isn't. I don't even know what you think Mercy and I will do for you. I honestly don't care. What I can tell you, no... *promise* you, is that I will spend every waking moment of my life making you miserable. I will never, ever give in. I'll make you kill me first. You're never going to get what you want from me."

Lucifer gave her a grim smile. Holding out a hand, he summoned a silver dagger, bringing it down to dangle above Mercy's head.

Vesper went very, very quiet and still.

"Any more you want to say?" Lucifer asked.

She was silent, but kept her head held high. Kirael had never felt so proud of another person in his entire existence. Sacrificing himself for Vesper's life was unquestionably right, she'd just confirmed it for him.

Only, it wasn't going to go quite the way he'd promised Lucifer.

"Right, then." Lucifer beckoned to Kirael. "Let's have the Book, and then you can go ahead and kneel, make it easy. I'm going to take your wings first, obviously."

"Obviously," Kirael said, holding out both hands to summon the Book.

Belial stepped forward, but Lucifer held up a hand. "No one touches the Book of Names but me."

Therein lay Lucifer's fatal flaw, laid bare for all to see.

Kirael moved forward, summoning a small dagger into his hand, under the Book. A very special dagger, something he'd been holding close for a long time.

It was a holy artifact from Kirael's earliest days, enchanted with the specific purpose of inflicting damage to the unrepentant. Today, all this time later, he finally had cause to use it to its fullest potential.

Lucifer stepped around Mercy, eager to reclaim his book of prophecies.

"Kirael!" Vesper cried.

Lucifer turned, just for a second, but it was enough. Kirael vanished the Book and struck out with the dagger, slicing Lucifer from shoulder to hip, deep and deadly.

Lucifer grunted, looking shocked. Black blood began to pour from the slash in his dark suit, hissing as it dribbled onto his clothes. Kirael dropped his blade, shaking off a few drops of blood as they began to burn his fingers.

"What *are* you?" he growled at Lucifer.

Lucifer fell, wounded and howling but very much alive. Kirael's heart lurched when he realized that he'd failed, that the dagger hadn't done nearly enough.

He turned just in time to see Belial bringing down his sword, aiming for Kirael's heart. An attempt to subdue him, in order to shear his wings and take his head. End him, forever.

The ground underfoot began to tremble. Belial stumbled, slicing at Kirael's shoulder. Kirael grabbed for his dagger, managing to get his fingers around the handle.

Then a dozen Fallen cried out, rushing toward Vesper. Kirael turned as Belial lunged at him again, his sword piercing Kirael's breast bone, just where Vesper had run him through before.

There was an unbelievable, ear-popping, awesomely loud roar. The ground shook harder, and Kirael managed to shove Belial to the ground. Dropping to his knees, he grappled with the sword, but it hit a spot that made his arm too weak to remove it.

Then he turned to look for Vesper, and his jaw dropped.

She was levitating, at least twenty feet in the air. Glowing, too — a bright, violent purple aura swirling all around her. Arms out at her sides, furious expression on her face, eyes gone a shade of violet that made all of the hair stand up on Kirael's body.

She was truly, utterly terrifying.

"Don't touch him!" she shrieked, pointing at the Fallen all around him.

One by one, they simply... collapsed.

Something clicked in the back of Kirael's brain. Lucifer thought her valuable, and she could drop Fallen with a mere thought...

"Holy Hell," he whispered. "She's a Fatale."

Behind him Belial gasped, scrambling backward until he found Mercy. He grabbed Mercy and held her up like a shield, which only made Vesper angrier. Vesper shrieked, the sound ringing through the air and bringing tears to Kirael's eyes.

The sound went on and on, Fallen dropping like sacks of flour. When at last it ended, Kirael could barely open his eyes. He glanced up, feeling wrung out, empty.

Vesper drifted down to the ground, graceful and calm as though she defeated the lords of Hell every single day of her life. She came over and put her hand on Kirael's shoulder. It felt cool, soothing, the way that his sword felt in his hand just before a battle.

"It's going to be okay," she told him, her voice back to normal though her eyes were still bright violet. "I'm going to take care of you, Kirael."

Kirael nodded. "Thank you."

His eyes closed, and he grunted when Vesper pulled the sword out of his shoulder.

"Just like old times, huh?" she asked him.

Kirael tried to laugh, but exhaustion overcame him. It hurt to breathe, it hurt to think. Between Belial and whatever Vesper did to everyone, he was going under...

He didn't resist, knowing Vesper would be there when he woke up.

24

VESPER

"Hey."

Vesper looked up from Kirael's couch, where she was catching up on some emails and Crane Co. documents. Kirael loomed in the doorway, wearing nothing but low slung pajama bottoms, his muscular torso bare except the bandages from his wound.

"Hey," she said, shutting her laptop. "There you are. I was starting to worry that you might not ever wake up."

"How long have I been out?" he asked, stretching.

Every muscle rippled, and Vesper bit her lip, averting her gaze. He was too much, almost. The heat and intensity of his gaze made her squirm.

"A whole day," she said, shuffling some papers.

Kirael came over and sat down beside her on the couch, wincing a little.

"Your shoulder still hurts, huh?" she asked.

"Like the devil himself." Kirael looked her up and down, making her blush. "How did we get here? I don't remember anything."

"Stella, if you can believe it. She showed up to see the aftermath of... me."

Kirael arched a brow, but didn't press her about the fact that she'd leveled a couple dozen Fallen all on her own. Instead, he kept the conversation light.

"I'm surprised Stella helped us."

"She was pretty cool, actually. I get the feeling that being around Lucan makes her more aggressive," Vesper said. "She snapped her fingers and took all three of us right to the portal."

"Wow," Kirael said, shaking his head. "I guess she's not as bad as I thought."

"She's something, all right," Vesper said. She hesitated, then said, "I need to talk to you about something."

"I'm listening," he said, pure patience.

"It's about the Null," she said.

His gaze narrowed. "Please don't tell me that you made that all up."

Vesper rolled her eyes.

"No, not at all. It's just... the Null is... someone I know."

"Well... that seems obvious," Kirael said.

"Right. What I'm trying to say is... I can't tell you who the Null is unless you promise me some things."

His brows shot up. "Like what?"

"Like... that being outed won't actually hurt h— them," Vesper said, correcting herself. "This... person... went to great lengths to hide what they are. There must be a reason."

"I assume... to avoid being captured and imprisoned by one side or the other."

"What? Lucifer kidnapping someone, I can see... but..." she said, glancing upward.

"Think of it like this. If someone takes the Null out of play, they have the exclusive chance to sway that person. Maybe it would be the most beautiful golden cage of all time, but either side would be crazy not to try. Consider the stakes."

Vesper looked at him for a long time, then slowly shook her head.

"I'm sorry, Kirael. If that's what's going to happen, I can't tell you who it is."

Kirael stared at her for several moments. Then he shocked the daylights out of her by shrugging. "Okay."

"That's it? No... righteous anger? I'm not holding up my end of the bargain!"

"Yeah, but you saved my life yesterday, so... call it even."

Vesper watched him closely, trying to tell if he was kidding.

"You're serious?"

"My hand to Heaven," he said, actually raising his hand. "I'm going to put my obsession with being forgiven on the back burner. Try just... being in one place for a while. Try being present, I guess."

"I... okay," she said, nodding. "Thank you for understanding."

He smiled, seemingly unconcerned. After a few beats, he changed the topic.

"Where's Mercy?"

"She's at Mere Marie's, on lockdown. She's going through withdrawals pretty bad, but Mere Marie is taking care of her. Gave her something to help her through the worst of it," Vesper said, silent for a moment. Then, "I can't get the image of her out of my head, the way she looked when I found her at the brothel. Kirael, it was so awful."

Kirael reached out and slid his arm around her. Vesper went willingly, leaning into his warmth and strength.

"She's going to be fine," Kirael promised.

Vesper made a disbelieving sound. "Right. This isn't exactly the first time I've rescued her. I've gotten her out before. I just can't make her get her act together. I can't *force* her to get clean, she has to want it. And if she's using, she'll end up right back where she was, or worse."

"What about rehab?" Kirael asked.

"Tried it, over and over. She doesn't want to be sober. And

now that Lucifer knows that we're... valuable... he'll be tempting her at every turn, I guarantee that."

Kirael looked thoughtful for a moment. "We should talk to Lucan. Maybe he can sway Stella into helping us on that front."

"You think that would help?" Vesper asked, laying her head on Kirael's shoulder.

"She has a surprising amount of pull with her father."

Vesper just nodded, unable to take it all in. "One step at a time."

Kirael looked away, perhaps gathering his thoughts. When he turned back to her, the look in his eyes took Vesper's breath away.

"Thank you," he said, putting his hand over hers.

"For what?" she asked, looking up at him.

"For saving my life," he said, giving her a look. "Not just back there in Hell, either."

"What do you mean?" Vesper said, her heart beginning to thrum in her chest.

"I just... for the longest time, I've been lost. Reliving the sins of my past, trying to find the will to escape Hell, desperate to regain Heaven's approval. I went from one big thing to another, and somewhere along the way I lost myself."

Vesper gave him a soft smile, turning her hand to squeeze his fingers.

"I understand perfectly," she said.

"I know. That's one of the things that makes you so unique," he said, brushing her hair back from her face. "It's why I care for you so deeply. Why I've fallen for you, so fast and so hard."

Vesper's mouth opened and closed, her face going tomato red.

"I... oh," was all she managed.

Kirael grinned. "You're good with words."

"You just surprised me, that's all!" she protested. "I don't really know how to talk about... feelings, and stuff."

"Me either. I'm trying to just say what I feel," he said, amused. "Is it working?"

Vesper smiled, feeling shy. "Yeah."

"This is the part where you tell me you've fallen for me, too," Kirael intoned.

Blushing to the roots of her hair, Vesper pulled a face. "Yes."

"Yes?" Kirael asked, teasing her now.

"Yes! Yes, Kirael. This is all still new to me, so… that's as much as you're going to get from me right this minute."

"I'll take it. Whatever you're willing to give me," Kirael said, leaning down to brush his lips against hers.

"Oh yeah?" she murmured.

"Mmmhm," he said, shifting so that he could nuzzle her jaw, her neck. "Have I told you that you smell amazing?"

"Do I?" she asked, her eyelids drifting shut as his lips touched the sweet spot at the base of her neck.

"Vanilla and spice," he said. "It's intoxicating."

"You smell like a pine forest," Vesper said, then laughed. "A sexy pine forest?"

Kirael grinned. "Whoa, easy on the dirty talk there, princess."

"Princess?" Vesper squeaked, pushing at him. "That is not a cute pet name."

"I like it," he said, tugging at the strap of her tank top, pulling it down to bare her shoulder.

The heat of his mouth against her skin made her shiver. "Mmm."

"Mmm, good? Mmmm, yes? Mmm, more, Kirael, please?" he asked, pressing another kiss to her collarbone.

"Yes. God, yes," Vesper said, shifting to get closer to him.

"Come here," he said, standing and picking her up.

"Kirael!" she cried as he threw her over his shoulder, carrying her down the hall to his bedroom.

It was cool and dark in the room, a perfect contrast to how

Vesper felt, hot and bright and excited. She squeaked when Kirael flung himself down on the bed, taking her with him.

His playfulness shocked her, made her laugh. His kiss, though... that stole her very breath. His lips on hers, his hands in her hair, his body a solid weight against hers. Making her feel small, but also protected. Safe.

Kirael stripped off her shirt, her jeans, and her bra. She was all but naked before him, her chest heaving as he knelt before her on the bed, looking at her with unquestionable hunger.

"God, Vesper. Look at you," he said, brushing his fingertips over the curve of her breast, the flat expanse of her stomach. "You're killing me."

Licking her lips, Vesper reached out to touch him, running her fingers over his hip, watching his expression intently.

"Wait..." she said.

Kirael gave her a look, but she shook her head.

"No, I just... can I see your wings?" she asked.

His lips twisted in a smirk. He closed his eyes for a second, and then there they were, his glorious white wings. He stretched them out fully, turning a little so that Vesper could examine them.

"Just for a moment," he said, watching her curiously.

Vesper rose to kneel next to him, reaching out. Her fingers trembled as she touched his left wing, the feathers downy and silken to the touch.

"They're so beautiful," she whispered, awed.

She ran her fingers along the delicate arch rising from his shoulder blade, and Kirael visibly shuddered.

"Is this okay?" she asked.

"It's unbearable, in the best way possible," he said, his eyes closing. He shivered, rolling his neck. He looked like a cat leaning into a friendly hand, enjoying her touch so deeply.

He stayed still, letting her explore for another minute. Then his eyes snapped open, his eyes dark and stormy.

"I need to touch you," he said, his wings vanishing. "I need you, Vesper."

He splayed a hand out over her lower back, pulling her flush against his body, heat rolling off him in waves. She turned her face up and he kissed her, teasing her lips apart, exploring her with deft strokes of his tongue.

Vesper's entire body tightened, heat pooling between her thighs. She brought Kirael's free hand to her breast and he shaped it, pinching her nipple until she moaned.

Kirael dragged her down, laying her out on the bed. He kissed her lips and her neck. He moved his fevered kisses to her bare shoulder. And when he laved his tongue over her sensitive nipple, she arched off the bed, her nails digging into his shoulders.

Kirael slid her panties down her legs, tossing them aside. His lips found her navel, then the gentle groove of her hip, and the juncture of one thigh. He nudged her knees apart, spreading her wide before his hungry gaze, and Vesper blushed as she let him, too hungry for him to be shy.

When Kirael lowered his mouth to her clit, teasing and hot, Vesper nearly shot off the bed, moaning and digging her fingers into his hair. His tongue and lips drove her wild, making her cry out his name and scratch at his shoulders. His steady masterful movements making her hips roll in a sultry rhythm.

"Kirael," she moaned, clutching the sheets. "I want more. I want you inside me. *Please*, Kirael."

His magical tongue left her body, which made her sigh. Soon enough, though, Kirael moved back up to kiss her, his hands roaming everywhere, driving her desire higher and higher.

"Kirael, please," she said again. "Now you're the one killing *me*."

He rose to strip off his pajama bottoms, giving Vesper a true eyeful. He was absolute perfection, circling his heavy erection with one hand as he paused to stare down at her.

"Come *here*," she insisted.

"Mmmm, I like it when you're bossy," he said, grasping his cock and bringing it to her core.

"I—" was all she got out, because Kirael filled her with a single, deep thrust. They both cried out, Vesper clinging to him as he began to work in and out of her body, satisfying her and frustrating her at once.

"Harder!" she said.

He slowed, teasing her, and she growled. When he withdrew, she shot him a dirty look.

"Relax, Vesper," he said with a grin. "Now get on your hands and knees."

Face going red, Vesper turned over, biting her lip as she wiggled her ass at him. Kirael got off the bed, standing up. He grabbed her hips and dragged her backward, standing between her calves.

He filled her again, fast and rough. Vesper let her face drop to the bed, groaning as he moved, the feel of him so perfect that it made her eyes roll up in her head.

"You feel so good," he told her, his fingers digging into her hips. "So, so good."

"Kirael... Kirael, I'm going to—" she whispered, then shattered, shouting her pleasure.

Kirael didn't slow, thrusting quick and hard as she shuddered and clenched around him. For several seconds, she was weightless, floating in the sweetness of it, sublime.

When she drifted back down, Kirael groaned, his movements growing brutal.

"Yes," she moaned, encouraging. "Let go."

He came with a low growl, filling her in sharp, deep thrusts. When he finally slowed and withdrew, they both collapsed with twin groans of exhausted satisfaction.

It took several long minutes before Vesper could move her limbs again. She contented herself with turning her face toward Kirael, watching his face. Eyes closed, hair sticking to his nape and jaw, he worked to catch his breath.

She knew Kirael would draw her close soon, but Vesper didn't want to wait.

This time, she wanted to be the one to make the first move, to show him how she felt.

Once she'd recovered a bit, Vesper moved closer, tucking her body against Kirael's. He slid an arm around her, his eyes opening for a brief moment, his lips turning up at the corners.

He looked so peaceful, Vesper did the exact same. Closing her eyes, she was content to lie next to him, just smiling like an idiot.

So, yeah. Maybe she wasn't great with the words. Maybe she was a little gun-shy.

Maybe this was all she could give him today, this little bit of herself. But she knew how she felt, deep down. She knew that Kirael was her perfect match. A *soulmate*, if you wanted to get corny about it.

The words would come, sooner rather than later, the pretty phrases that made hearts skip a beat. Kirael would be right there, when she was brave enough to say them all.

For now, this was... *perfect*.

25

KIRAEL

Kirael lay quietly and feigned sleep, waiting for Vesper to drift off.

All he wanted to do was fall asleep holding her, but there was something he needed to do first. Once he was absolutely sure that she was out cold, he gently rolled Vesper onto her back. Getting up, he covered her with a blanket before grabbing some clothes.

This is a little too familiar, he thought. *This time I'm coming back before she wakes up, though.*

Considering what he was about to do, Vesper would no doubt forgive his short absence. His words to her earlier were true, though: he did intent to be present, to give up his obsessive search for penitence.

For Vesper, for himself. This would only be the firming of his resolution. Though the idea had only come to him as he lay in bed with Vesper, inhaling her sweet scent, he knew it was the right thing to do.

He was down the stairs in a matter of minutes, out in the still-humid New Orleans night air. There was nothing for it, this close to the bayou. Locals just got used to the way everything stuck to their skin, the dampness of it all.

Heading straight down to Jackson Square, he scanned the moonlit pedestrian walkway in front of the Cathedral. Across the way, he spotted a scraggly-looking figure pushing a shopping cart full of soda cans, covered head to toe in a heavy, hooded coat despite the weather.

"There you are," he said, mostly to himself.

Kirael made a beeline for the man, waiting until he got a few paces away to call out, "Arturos!"

The figure slowed, glanced back. Even from here, in the dark, Kirael could tell that Arturos wasn't close to looking human. The odd Fae creature blinked big yellow eyes at Kirael, looking like a startled owl.

For the life of him, Kirael couldn't figure out how Arturos passed every manner of human, all day and all night, and no one ever found him out. Arturos leaned forward, his long white beak appearing in the moonlight.

It was the most of Arturos that Kirael had ever actually seen.

"Call Arturos?" the Fae asked, his voice like the creaking of a thousand tree branches. His beak clicked when he spoke, and for some reason the clicking itself made all Kirael's hair stand on end, a sure sign of a dangerous creature.

"Yes. I have a trade," Kirael said, determined.

Arturos didn't move for a long time. When he inclined his head, Kirael let out a breath he didn't know he'd been holding.

"What trade?" Arturos asked.

Kirael held out both his palms and closed his eyes, summoning the Book of Names. When he looked up, he could see nearly all of Arturos's beak, and the tip of his pointy white chin.

"Book. Have Book," Arturos clicked. "Trade Book."

"Yes," Kirael said.

"Give Book. What Trade."

"You want to know what I need in exchange?"

Arturos dipped his head. "What Trade, Angel."

Angel. It had been so long since anyone had called Kirael that, the word took him off-guard.

"There is a girl, a woman. She is at Mere Marie's house. Do you know the place?" he asked.

Another dip of Arturos's head.

"She is sick. Drugs, who knows what. I need her to stop."

Arturos was still. "Change Girl Heart?"

It took him a moment to parse that. "Yes, that's what I'm asking. I want you to change what's in her heart, make her want to get better. Can you do that?"

Silence. Painful, terrible silence. Then, "Give Book. Trade Book. Girl Want."

"Yes," Kirael said, his relief immense. Then he hesitated. "And one more thing."

"Want."

It was impulsive, but... "A ring. From Keil's on Royal Street."

"Ring."

"It's a canary diamond with some kind of sapphires. Massive. Used to belong to Mary Queen of Scots or something."

Arturos blinked his big owl eyes. "Ring. Trade."

"You will heal Mercy, from the inside out. And deliver the ring to me, sooner than later. And in exchange, I will give you the book. Do we have a deal?"

He couldn't see much past the very tip of Arturos's beak, but Kirael could've sworn that the Fae *smiled*.

"Trade. Deal."

Kirael held out the book, wondering what Arturos's hands looked like. He'd never know, though; Arturos crumbled like a column of ash, a sudden brisk wind sweeping him into a swirl of air.

In a blink, the swirl covered the book. In the next instant, Kirael's hands were empty. Before him, Arturos's shopping cart stood, abandoned.

"Okay..." Kirael said, shaking his head. "I suppose we're done, then."

Turning back toward his flat, Kirael couldn't stop the smile on his lips.

Vesper. He was already imagining crawling back into bed with her, the sleepy sound she might make, the feel of her body pressed against him.

Since the moment of the Fall, he'd been ungrounded, lost.

For the first time since that terrible moment, Kirael knew exactly who he was, where he was going. He was going to be with Vesper, and though the apartment itself meant almost nothing to him, a singular thought rang though every fiber of his being.

He wasn't going to a particular place. Rather, he was going to where *she* was.

Kirael was going *home*.

EPILOGUE

esper - Six Months Later

VESPER LACED her fingers with Kirael's, swinging their hands between them as they walked. He nodded at a bunch of ducks flying overhead, a common enough sight in City Park.

"I don't get your thing with birds," she said.

He just winked and shrugged, unworried as they continued their stroll, cutting across one big corner of the park.

"I like this walk," he said. "It's nice to get off the Canal Streetcar, then see a little of the park, and then there's Vargus's house."

"Yep. It's pretty amazing," Vesper agreed, although they both knew she wasn't talking about the location.

They made it to Vargus's a few minutes later. A familiar figure sat on the front stoop of Vargus's little shotgun, head down, intent on…

"Are you shelling peas?" Vesper called as they crossed the yard.

Mercy's head snapped up, and she grinned. "Yep. They just came out of my garden last night."

"Ridiculous," Vesper said. She eyed her sister; Mercy's dark hair was growing long and dark and pretty. She was finally filling out a little, too. More chic model and less skeleton lady.

It was a sight that Vesper had never thought to see again. Each time she laid eyes on the new, improved, sober Mercy, she wanted to kiss Kirael on the mouth. Well, she always wanted to kiss him, but this was a special kind of grateful, thank-you kiss.

After all, he'd made this happen. Mercy had been the one to struggle through the withdrawal and continued therapy sessions, but... none of it would have been possible if Kirael hadn't given up the Book of Names.

She glanced at Kirael, squeezed his hand, and then reluctantly released him. Just for a minute, just to hug her sister.

Good god I am so clingy lately, she thought with a sigh.

Mercy set the peas aside, rising and brushing her hands off on her apron. She opened her arms, beckoning to Vesper. "C'mere."

They hugged, Vesper's heart starting to overflow. When she stepped back, she had to blot at her eyes, trying not to sniff.

"What's wrong with you?" Mercy said, giving Vesper the eye.

Vesper flushed. "Nothing. Just... emotional. You know. I'm just... I'm so glad that you're here, and..."

"Oh, don't start crying," Mercy sighed, patting her on the shoulder. "Kirael, what's up with her?"

Vesper glanced at Kirael, who merely raised a brow and a shoulder at once, unconcerned. "Not a thing, as far as I can see."

Vesper blushed even harder. "Quit."

"I like it when you get red in the face," he said. "No shame here."

"Vargus!" Mercy yelled over her shoulder. "They're here!"

Vargus bent low to poke his head out the front door. "Bout time. I'm starving."

"Ugh, werewolves," Mercy said, flapping a hand. "You ever

want a roommate who will eat you out of house and home, a werewolf'll do the trick."

"I will remind you that I own this property," Vargus said, amused.

Mercy paid him no mind, turning back to Vesper. "You look dead tired. You could have called to cancel, you know. Did you work late?"

Vesper glanced at Kirael, feeling a dumb smile creep over her face. That was her life now, thrilled one minute, crying the next, then back to thrilled. It was like her heart was on a roller coaster, every waking second.

Kirael just nodded at her. Vesper fiddled with her ring, feeling self-conscious.

"I'm going to take some time off, actually."

Mercy had turned to head back inside, but now she paused. She came back around slowly, looking suspicious. "Why?"

"Well, because... I won't be able to work. For about seven more months, and then a while after that," Vesper said, pulling a face.

"Or never," Kirael chimed in.

Vesper raised a hand, shutting him down. He'd wanted her to quit her job from day one, this was just more incentive for him to insist.

"Wh— oh. Ohhhhh," Mercy said, pressing her fingers to her mouth. She looked at Kirael, who nodded. "Oh, really?"

"Really, what?" Vargus asked, leaning against the door frame.

"A baby, Vargus," Mercy said, giving him a look.

Vargus's jaw dropped, which made Vesper crack up.

"You— really?" he asked, echoing Mercy.

"Yes, really!" Vesper said. "People have babies, Vargus. It's a thing."

His shock was comical, but not as comical perhaps as the way Vesper's own mouth dropped open when Vargus grabbed Mercy by the waist, swinging her up, and then kissed her.

"Oh, put me down," Mercy said, sounding flustered. Now it was Mercy's turn to blush, it seemed.

Vesper was sure she must look the very picture of surprise, right then.

"Wait, are you two..." she asked, pointing back and forth between Vargus and Mercy.

"Oh, hush, don't worry about us," Mercy declared. "Now come inside and sit down to dinner. I want to hear every single detail."

"Okay, okay!" Vesper said with a laugh.

"I mean it, Ves. You never listen to me, but you'd better listen to me now..." Mercy said, her voice trailing off as she headed inside.

Vargus followed her, leaving Kirael and Vesper alone for a final moment before dinner.

They looked at each other, grinned, and kissed one more time. Then Kirael took her hand, leading her inside to dinner — and a truly happy *family* meal.

ALSO BY KAYLA GABRIEL

Alpha Guardians

See No Evil

Hear No Evil

Speak No Evil

Bear Risen

Bear Razed

Bear Reign

Alpha Guardians Boxed Set

———

Red Lodge Bears

Luke's Obsession

Noah's Revelation

Gavin's Salvation

Cameron's Redemption

Josiah's Command

Finn's Conviction

Wyatt's Resolution

———

Werewolf's Harem

Claimed by the Alpha - 1

Taken by the Pack - 2

Possessed by the Wolf - 3

Saved by the Alpha - 4

Forever with the Wolf - 5

Fated for the Wolf - 6

<u>Winter Lodge Wolves</u>

Howl

Growl

Prowl

GET A FREE BOOK!

Join my mailing list to be the first to know of new releases, free books, special prices and other author giveaways.

http://freeshifterromance.com

ABOUT THE AUTHOR

Kayla Gabriel lives in the wilds of Minnesota where she swears she sees shifters in the woods beyond her yard. Her favorite things in life are mini marshmallows, coffee and when people use their blinker.

Connect with Kayla by
email: kaylagabrielauthor@gmail.com and be sure to get her FREE book: freeshifterromance.com

http://kaylagabriel.com

www.ingramcontent.com/pod-product-compliance
Lightning Source LLC
LaVergne TN
LVHW011823060526
838200LV00053B/3877